T0063750

WOMEN OF THE
HARLEM RENAISSANCE

More American classics by women writers
from Macmillan Collector's Library

WOMEN OF THE HARLEM RENAISSANCE

Poems & Stories

With an introduction by
KATE DOSSETT

Edited by
MARISSA CONSTANTINOU

MACMILLAN COLLECTOR'S LIBRARY

This collection first published 2022 by Macmillan Collector's Library
an imprint of Pan Macmillan
The Smithson, 6 Briset Street, London ECIM 5NR
EU representative: Macmillan Publishers Ireland Ltd, 1st Floor,
The Liffey Trust Centre, 117–126 Sheriff Street Upper,
Dublin 1, DOI YC43
Associated companies throughout the world
www.panmacmillan.com

ISBN 978-1-5290-6922-8

Selection and arrangement copyright
© Macmillan Publishers International Limited 2022

Introduction copyright © Kate Dossett 2022

The permissions acknowledgements on p. 201 constitute an
extension of this copyright page.

1 3 5 7 9 8 6 4 2

A CIP catalogue record for this book is available from the British Library.

Casing design and endpaper pattern by Andrew Davidson
Typeset by Jouve (UK), Milton Keynes
Printed and bound in China by Imago

Visit **www.panmacmillan.com** to read more
about all our books and to buy them.

*To all the women, from all walks of life,
breaking down barriers to opportunity*

Contents

vii

Introduction

KATE DOSSETT

If any have a song to sing
That's different from the rest,
Oh let them sing

'To Usward', Gwendolyn Bennett

Gwendolyn Bennett stands ready, waiting to deliver her glorious call to song. The night is 21 March 1924, the venue, the Civic Club in New York City, and the occasion, a party Bennett has organized with Regina Andrews to celebrate the publication of Jessie Fauset's first novel, *There is Confusion*. Initiated by and for women creatives, nevertheless the evening would come to be remembered as the party that launched the literary careers of a 'younger group' of male writers. Hosted by Charles S. Johnson, editor of the journal *Opportunity*, with Howard University professor Alain Locke serving as toast-master, the conversations that took place that night between Black creatives and white publishing houses led to a special 'Black' edition of the magazine *Survey Graphic* (March 1925), expanded to a book-length collection, *The New Negro*, which was published later the same year. Edited by Locke, these anthologies have come to define the Harlem Renaissance, featuring poems, essays, short fiction and artwork by some of the movement's shining stars: Langston Hughes, Claude McKay, Zora Neale Hurston and Jean Toomer. However, the two volumes capture only a partial view of debates about race, gender and sexuality that animated the Harlem Renaissance. One reason for this is that women are poorly represented across the two publications: just four of the twenty-four contributors to *Survey Graphic*, and eight of the forty authors featured in *The New Negro* are women. Anthologies are important in determining who gets remembered, whose ideas matter and how we understand our pasts. They are part of a broader knowledge-producing industry in America, one long controlled by white and usually male Americans. Anthologies confer legitimacy on certain writers while excluding others. They record what a particular group of editors, scholars and publishers thought worth preserving at a particular moment in time and who had the power to make these decisions. As such, they are always contested terrain, for they exist alongside multiple alternative versions that never made it into print.

This anthology of poems and short stories celebrates a different version of the Harlem Renaissance, one that begins with and is sustained by the work of Black women. As artists, poets, playwrights, singers, composers, essayists and activists, women understood themselves to be at the heart of the movement we now call the Harlem Renaissance. Concentrated in but not limited to the neighbourhood of Harlem in upper Manhattan, contemporaries often referred to the increased opportunities for publication, exhibition and performance as the 'New Negro' movement. Not only in New York but in Boston, Chicago and Washington DC, Black artists, writers, musicians and activists explored new ways of expressing their experiences of race, gender and sexuality in modern America. Later, scholars debated when the movement began, and when it came to an end. Many agree it grew in strength through the late 1910s, developed in purpose and possibility through the 1920s and should be extended to include the 1930s. While the thirties have long been viewed as after the peak of the Renaissance, these were the years when many women finally were able to find publishers for their novels and space to exhibit their artwork.

The Harlem Renaissance was a movement that was intimately connected to the expansion of the commercial music industry. The Jazz Age offered unprecedented opportunities for Black musicians to perform in live venues across the United States, before segregated and sometimes mixed audiences. Meanwhile millions of Americans gathered around gramophones in their homes and communal spaces, where they could play over and again the records that captured the powerful voices of Bessie Smith and Ma Rainey. Whether as blues singers, writers or artists, women did not experience access to these new platforms on the same terms as men and the rewards were seldom distributed equally. The very networks and systems that supported artistic production by men often held back the careers of women: lousy recording contracts, fewer opportunities for publication and to win prizes, fellowships and grants. Then there was the hard-to-quantify, but often devastating, assortment of slights and oversights: the invitations that never arrived, the reviews not written, all of which made it more difficult for women to sustain careers as writers and artists.

Black women's writing did not begin with the Harlem Renaissance. African American women have always expressed their desires, narrated their histories and articulated their vision for a better world through a variety of oral, visual and written forms. However, it was in the first decades of the twentieth century that

Black women were increasingly able to access and create new platforms from which their voices could be heard. The mass migration of African Americans from the rural South towards urban centres in the North and West reached its peak in the 1920s and 1930s. Determined to find a more meaningful freedom than that offered by sharecropping and segregation, and in resistance to the white mob violence that denied Black men their constitutional right to vote and Black women their sexual autonomy, many Black southerners looked for liberty in the cities of the North. Black women and men migrated in significant numbers to Chicago, New York City, Philadelphia, Detroit and Pittsburgh. As in the South, domestic service remained one of the primary avenues of employment for Black women migrating to northern cities. However, the labour shortages created when the US government drafted men to fight in World War I opened up more lucrative jobs in factories, in the garment industry, as well as in nursing, social work and education. Black women also found employment in the burgeoning entertainment and nightlife industries that sprang up in many northern cities. With new opportunities to spend leisure time and money away from the ties of home and oppressive southern race relations, women embraced and helped birth an awakening of Black expressive culture. In clubs, church halls, concert venues, bars and theatres, female artists sought to redefine how they were seen and heard. Blues singers sang about same-sex desire and domestic violence; theatre makers dramatized Black women's experiences of lynching and motherhood; writers gave voice to intersectional experiences, captured brilliantly in Marita Bonner's 1925 essay 'On Being Young—A Woman—And Colored'.

Black urban neighbourhoods were also enriched by broader demographic patterns shaping American cities in the early decades of the twentieth century. Driven by crippling poverty at home, growing kinship networks and employment opportunities in the United States, Caribbean immigrants were attracted to all the major cities of the Atlantic seaboard, and especially New York City. In 1930, 65 per cent of the foreign-born Black population of the United States lived in New York City, where they constituted 16.7 per cent of all Black residents. Coming from Black-majority countries, Caribbean-born activists brought to the city new ideas and perspectives on how to defeat global white supremacy, whether in Jim Crow America or the powerful European empires in Africa and Asia. Preaching 'Race First', activists such as Amy Jacques Garvey and her husband Marcus Garvey, who led the Universal Negro Improvement Association (UNIA), the largest mass Black movement in US history, were part of a global pan-African movement that spurred new forms of Black cultural expression. Overlapping with and extending the themes of the American Harlem Renaissance was the Négritude movement, a literary and political movement developed by Francophone African and Caribbean Black intellectuals living in Paris who would later become influential figures in ending colonial governments in Africa. Black women writing during the Harlem Renaissance frequently penned poems expressing solidarity with peoples of African descent across the globe. Many were published in the leading Black nationalist paper of the day, the UNIA's *Negro World*, which Amy Ashwood Garvey (Marcus Garvey's first wife) set up with her husband in New York City in 1917. However, the poems of Carrie

Williams Clifford published in this anthology remind us that women had been writing odes to Black solidarity before the Jamaican Garveys came to Harlem. Clifford published two collections of poems (*Race Rhymes*, 1911, and *The Widening Light*, 1922) expressing the determination of Black Americans to fight for their rights at home and abroad. Published ten years apart and included in this collection, 'Silent Protest Parade' and 'We'll Die for Liberty' capture a sense of common purpose and dignity held close by those fighting for Black freedom across the globe.

Connecting to a global Black community was a prominent theme of a movement whose famous sons travelled across the African diaspora. Claude McKay and Langston Hughes explored how race was made in Europe and Africa, documenting their international adventures in memoirs and drawing on their experiences in their poetry and fiction. The experience of global travel was not available to most women writers: caring and financial responsibilities often kept them closer to home. Jessie Fauset and Gwendolyn Bennett were two who did travel and write about their time abroad studying in Paris; others made connections through pan-Africanist and clubwomen's networks, hosting women from across the diaspora and expanding their vision of global Black solidarity. Whether or not they travelled abroad, the desire to break free from the 'narrowest nest' is a recurring theme in women's writing, as we see in this anthology. Georgia Douglas Johnson's narrator in the poem 'Your World' yearns 'To travel this immensity'. For Jessie Fauset's heroine in 'The Sleeper Wakes', a bigger life requires leaving behind her loving adopted Black family in Trenton, New

Jersey, and reinventing herself with a white identity in New York City.

Escape, especially from the burdens of Black parenthood, is a prominent theme in women's writing. Angelina Weld Grimké's drama *Rachel* (1916) is perhaps the best-known example of a Black feminist writer articulating the horror of bringing Black children into a world that would dehumanize them, but women explore the cost of motherhood in poems and short fiction too. In Johnson's 'Motherhood' (initially published in *The Crisis* magazine and later included in her self-published collection *Bronze*, under the more inclusive title, 'Black Woman') the narrator tells her imagined future child 'Don't knock at my heart, little one, / I cannot bear the pain'. The 'monster men' she describes here haunt the poems and short fiction produced by other Harlem Renaissance writers featured in this anthology: the white lynch mob, the white sheriff, the white youth whose attraction to and fear of Black men cannot be spoken. Against these spectres Black parents are often powerless. In the stories 'Nothing New' (Marita Bonner) and 'Sanctuary' (Nella Larsen), and the poem 'An Apostrophe to the Lynched' (Lelia Amos Pendleton), the author explores the dangers which haunt the journey from childhood to maturity, especially for Black men.

Across the collection we see a desire to represent Black women's voices by attending to their actual words. Many of the stories by women published in *The Crisis* and *Opportunity* employ rural folk dialect. The scholar June Jordan has argued that the articulation of Black English is an important part of preserving Black culture and history, a theme brilliantly on show in Pendleton's 'The Foolish and the Wise'. Female relationships also feature prominently in women's writing, including the differing experiences of white and Black women, as well as the sometimes-difficult relationships between mothers and their daughters, a generation or more removed from slavery. Women admiring women's bodies and the desire for beauty is featured in women's verse, captured here in 'Heritage', Bennett's sensuous celebration of Black girlhood in the opening poem of the collection.

This volume offers a glimpse of the breadth and diversity of women's writing during the Renaissance. Although their work was often excluded from anthologies produced at the time, we are able to access it now because of the brilliant recovery work of Black feminist scholars over the last fifty years, as well as the labour of women editors and writers who promoted and published each other's work in Black-led journals and magazines during the Renaissance. Many of the pieces that appear in this collection were first published in Black-led journals, including *Opportunity*, *The Crisis* and *Colored American* magazine, where women took on major editorial roles and used their power to increase the visibility of and audience for women's writing. Judith Musser, who has edited two anthologies of women's writing published in Harlem Renaissance periodicals, estimates that 135 short stories by African American women were published in *Opportunity* and *The Crisis* between 1923 and 1948, with women making up close to 50 per cent of all short stories published across the two journals. Women were also well represented as poets. Of the 624 poems published across the two journals between 1918 and 1931 where gender can be identified, the literary and women's studies scholar Maureen Honey calculates that 277 were by women.

Republishing women's short-form fiction and poetry from these journals and from women's self-published collections offers us a different lens through which to view this vibrant moment in Black letters and its legacy for American culture today.

To return to Gwendolyn Bennett, poised to deliver her new poem at the Civic Club. She has to wait until the very end, until all the other speakers are introduced, and after Fauset has finally been allowed to say a few words. Eventually the platform is hers. She uses it to celebrate those with songs to sing that are 'different from the rest'. This ode to Black creative possibility she dedicates to Fauset, who will publish it in the next edition of *The Crisis* (May 1924). The networks, creativity and ambition of Black women writers in the Harlem Renaissance helped them endure rejection, find alternative avenues to publication and keep on keeping on. Their struggle and achievements inspire a new generation of Black women artists to sing from a larger stage and paint from a broader canvas. Amanda Gorman, America's first National Youth Poet Laureate, celebrated this legacy when she delivered *The Hill We Climb* at the inauguration of the forty-sixth American president and of the first woman and first person of colour to the office of vice president in January 2021. Like the work collected here, Gorman's poem reminds us of her nation's flawed past and uncertain future; but hers is also a poem of hope, one built on firm foundations and a confidence that the freedom dreams of Black women can make change happen, 'if only we're brave enough to see it'.

WOMEN OF THE
HARLEM RENAISSANCE

Gwendolyn B. Bennett

Heritage

I want to see the slim palm-trees,
Pulling at the clouds
With little pointed fingers . . .

I want to see lithe Negro girls
Etched dark against the sky
While sunset lingers.

I want to hear the silent sands,
Singing to the moon
Before the Sphinx-still face . . .

I want to hear the chanting
Around a heathen fire
Of a strange black race.

I want to breathe the Lotus flow'r,
Sighing to the stars
With tendrils drinking at the Nile . . .

I want to feel the surging
Of my sad people's soul,
Hidden by a minstrel-smile.

First published in the journal
Opportunity (December 1923)

Summer Session

"You were flirting with him!"

"I was not. I don't know how to flirt."

"So you say, but you can put up a pretty good imitation."

"You're mistaken."

"I am not. And a man you never saw before in your life. And a common taxi driver."

"He's not a common taxi driver."

"How do you know?"

"I just know."

"Strange exchange of intimacies for the first meeting."

"I tell you—"

"Shut up!"

"I won't shut up, and don't you dare tell me that again!"

There was a warning note in her usually gentle voice; an ominous tightening of her soft lips; a steely glint in her violet eyes. Logan heeded the warning and sat in grim silence, while Elise ground gears and otherwise mishandled her little car through the snarled traffic of Amsterdam Avenue.

"You told me 114th Street, and I waited for you there for a half hour, and I got jammed in the traffic and things went wrong, and this young man got out of his taxi, and straightened me out. And while I waited for you he just stayed and talked."

"To your delight."

"What was I to do? Push him away from the running board? I was standing still, and I couldn't drive away since I was waiting for you."

"I told you 115th Street, and there I stood on the corner in the broiling sun for a half hour, while you were carrying on a flirtation with a taxi driver, until I walked back, thinking you might have had an accident."

"Don't you say flirtation to me again. You said 114th Street. You never speak plain over the telephone anyhow."

"Anything else wrong with me since you've met your new friend—The Taxi Adonis?"

Elise brought the car to a grinding, screeching pause in front of the movie house which was their objective. They sat through the two hours of feature and news and cartoons and comedy and prevues in stony silence. They ate a grim meal together in the usual cafeteria, and she set him down at the men's dormitory of the university in the same polite and frigid silence. Logan glanced at her now and then just a trifle apprehensively. He had never seen just this trace of hardness in her, like the glint of unexpected steel beneath soft chiffon. But his manly dignity would not permit him to unbend. He answered her cold good-night with one as cold, and for the first time in that summer session, during which they had grown to know and like one another, they parted without making a future date.

He waited for her next day at luncheon hour, as she came from her class with a half dozen other chattering summer-school teacher-students. His manner was graciously condescending.

"Shall we have luncheon together?" Lordly and superior as usual.

3

She flashed her usual violet-eyed smile of delight, but he felt, rather than saw, that the smile did not quite reach the eyes; that the violets were touched as by premature frost.

"What I can't quite understand," he pursued, after he had brought her tray, deftly removed the salad, tea, and crackers, and placed the tray behind the next chair, "is, if you are skillful enough to drive from Portland, Maine, to New York alone and without disaster, how you can get mixed up in a mere traffic jam on Amsterdam Avenue, and have to have a taxi driver get you out."

Elise's brows went up at the awkward English, so at variance with his usual meticulous and precise phrasing, and a haunting query clouded her eyes. Logan quenched an embarrassed "Hem" in iced tea.

"I did not drive from Portland," was her final response. "I came from my own town, twenty-seven miles beyond Portland."

There was no particular reason for Elise's driving down Amsterdam Avenue after classes that afternoon, but she did and a friendly red light brought her to a halt at 114th Street. Adonis—Logan's sneering cognomen stuck in her mind, and she realized with a guilty start how ruggedly applicable it was—stuck his face in her car window. Poppies suffused her cheeks and dewey violets swam in a sea of flame.

"All right?" he queried.

"Quite, thank you." The light was happily yellow, and she meshed her gears.

"What's the hurry?" He put a protesting hand on the wheel.

"I have an engagement!" She sped away frantically. Adonis whistled at the wabbling career of her little coupé down the street.

4

She saw him just ahead of her in the cafeteria line next evening at dinner time. She reached for her tray with hands that insisted upon trembling, though she shook them angrily. He smiled daringly back at her. He was even handsomer out of his taxi uniform than in it, and the absence of the cap revealed crisp auburn curls of undoubted pugnaciousness.

"You get a seat, I'll bring your dinner."

"But I—"

"Go on—"

There was a difference between Adonis' ordering of her movements and that of Logan's. A sureness of merry audacity against prim didacticism. She sat at a window table and meekly arranged silver napkins.

"But I could never eat all that," she protested at the tray. "Beef and potatoes and—and—all that food."

"I knew that's what's the trouble—diet of salads and iced tea and crackers, mentally, spiritually, physically."

Elise ate roast beef and corn on the cob and pie à la mode and laughed at Adonis' jokes, and his whimsical descriptions of man and his appetites. Over their cigarettes she chuckled at his deft characterizations of their fellow diners.

"Eat hay and think hay," he was saying, "thin diets and thin souls. You need a red-blooded chap like me to make you eat food, put flesh on your bones and reconstruct your thinking from New England inhibitions to New York acceptance and enjoyment of life."

Elise's world rocked. School principals used muddled English. Taxi drivers talked like college professors.

Adonis paused and regarded something on his shoulder as if it were a tarantula. Logan's hand quivered in rage, and veins stood up on its pallor "like long blue whips," Elise found herself thinking.

5

"Aren't you taking a lot of liberties with a young lady to whom you've not been introduced?" snarled the owner of pallor and veins.

Adonis brushed off the hand and the remark with a careless gesture. He arose and bowed elaborately. "Miss Stone and I have been introduced, thank you, by ourselves—and you?"

Elise looked perilously near tears, "Oh, er—Logan—Mr. Long—this is—er—Mr. McShane."

Logan looked stonily through Adonis, "I don't accept introductions to taxi drivers, even if you do eat with them, Elise."

"Oh, please—" she began.

"That's all right," Adonis gathered up the checks. "Just let me settle this with the cashier, and then if you don't mind, we'll go outside, and settle the physical difference between a taxi driver and—" He did not finish the sentence, but the sinister drawl and contemptuous pause made Elise's scalp prickle with shame for Logan.

"You would suggest a common brawl; quite true to type. I hope, Elise, you have seen enough of such ruffianly conduct to be satisfied."

"Quite the contrary," she answered cooly, "I am going out with Mr. McShane in his taxi." It was pure spite, and she had a sinking feeling that she might not be wanted.

"Terry to you," he retorted, "and let's be going. We've got a busy evening before us."

Logan was beside them on the sidewalk, blocking the way to the taxi parked at the curb.

"Elise, don't be a fool." He grasped her arm and wrenched it, so that she gave an involuntary cry of pain. Terence McShane's next three moves were so violently

6

consecutive as to seem simultaneous. His right hand caught Logan neatly on the point of the chin, so that he went down with amazing swiftness; his left encircled Elise's waist and lifted her into the taxi, and both hands swung the machine with a roar and sputter in the general direction of the Washington bridge.

"But you're losing fares," Elise protested.

"Nonsense. If you can stand this bumpety-bump, what's the dif?"

"It's entrancing," she murmured at the river, the sky, the stars, the electric signs on the Jersey shore, at Terry's hatless curls.

"Police call," the radio protested, "calling all police cars. Look out for taxi license Y327D. Driver abducted summer school student. Watch for taxi. Arrest driver. Kidnapping charge."

From their leafy shelter, where somehow the taxi had parked itself—neither could have told when or how it stopped under those particularly umbrageous trees, they stared at the radio's accusing dial.

"Well, I'll be—" Terry swore softly. "What do you think of that worm putting in such a charge at headquarters?"

"Oh, Terry, you'll be arrested and put in jail!"

"Will you go to jail with me?"

"You know I will—oh, what am I saying?"

"Words of wisdom, me darlin'. Let's go. Anyhow I'm glad we didn't cross the bridge and get into Jersey."

Through circuitous ways and dark streets, avoiding police, taxis, inquisitive small boys and reporters on the loose, they drew up in front of police headquarters.

Elise sat demurely on a bench, and began to repair damages to her hair, complexion, and neck frills. The little pocket mirror wavered ever so slightly as Logan

7

stood accusingly in front of her, but her eyes did not leave the scrutiny of their mirrored counterpart.

"A pretty mess you've made of your life and reputation," he thundered. "Your chances for any position in my school are gone."

Elise put back a refractory curl behind her ear, then tried it out on her cheek again, surveying it critically in the mirror.

"Won't you recommend me for a job, Mr. Principal, after I've studied so hard all summer?"

Terry's gales of unrestrained mirth at the desk made them both look up in amazement. Laughter rocked the walls of the station house, rolled out into the summer street. Captain and Sergeant and Lieutenant and just plain officers roared lustily, all save one quiet plainclothes man, who laid an iron grip on Logan's arm.

"Terence McShane, you were always the best detective in the city," roared the Captain. "And you made him bring himself right into our outstretched arms."

The iron grip on Logan's arm terminated into steel bracelets.

"Okeh, Longjim Webb, alias Prof. Logan Long, the school principal, looking the summer students over for teaching material in his consolidated upstate school, we'll give you a chance in the Big House to meditate on the law against white slavery."

"Your zeal to corral this particular choice bit of femininity made you throw caution to the winds," suggested Detective Terrence McShane.

Incredulity, disgust, anger swept the violet eyes. Elise flared into Terry's face.

"You—you—pretending to be a taxi driver. You just used me for a decoy," she raged.

8

Terry held her protesting hands tight as he whispered below the hubbub of Logan's protestations,

"Never a bit of it, my dear. I loved you the first day you stalled your car in the thick of things on 125th Street, before you even saw me, and I got in the habit of following you around while I was impersonating a taxi driver, to get a chance to know you. Then when I found this—" a wave towards the still-voluble Logan—"had marked you for another one of his prey— well you don't mind if I combined a bit of business with my pleasure?"

Elise's faint "No" was visible, rather than audible.

"It's all right then? Shall it be beefsteak for two?"

"Yes."

"And you won't take back what you promised up there on the Drive?"

"How can I," she laughed, "when my middle name is McBride?"

Unpublished (*c.* 1928–1932)

Gerarda

The day is o'er and twilight's shade,
Is darkening forest, glen and glade;
It steals within the old church door,
And casts its shadows on the floor;
It throws its gloom upon the bride,
And on her partner by her side:
But ah! it has no power to screen
The loveliest form that e'er was seen.

Sweet tones as from the angels' lyre,
Came pealing from the ancient choir;
They rouse the brain with magic power,
And fill with light that twilight hour.
Some artist's soul one easily sees,
Inspires the hands that touch the keys;
A genius sits and wakes the soul,
With sounds that o'er the passions roll.

"Till death we part," repeats the bride.
She shuddered visibly and sighed;
And as she leaves the altar rail,
She's startled, and her features pale,
For in the ancient choir above,
The man who sits and plays of love,
Has held her heart for many a year.
Alas! her life is sad and drear.

He never dreamed he roused a thrill,
Within that heart that seemed so still;

He never knew the hours of pain,
That racked that tired and troubled brain.
He could not see that bleeding heart,
From which his face would not depart;
He never could have known her grief,
From which, alas! there's no relief.

At last she thought the fire had cooled,
And love's strong guardian she had ruled;
'Twas then she vowed to be the bride
Of him who stands at her side.
Ill-fated hour! she sees too late,
This man she cannot help but hate;
He, whom she promised to obey,
Until from earth she's called away.

This life is sometimes dark and drear,
No lights within the gloom appear.
Gerarda smiled and danced that night,
As though her life had been all bright;
And no one knew a battle waged,
Within that heart so closely caged.
The few who've never felt love's dart,
Know not the depth of woman's heart.

II

Gerarda sat one summer day,
With easel, brush, and forms of clay,
Within her much-loved studio,
Where all that makes the senses glow
Were placed with great artistic skill;
Content, perhaps, she seems, and still,

She'd give this luxury and more,
To ease that heart so bruised and sore.

Her paintings hang upon the wall,
The power of genius stamps them all;
On this material soil she breathes,
But in her spiritual word she leaves
Her mind, her thoughts, her soul, her brain,
And wakes from fancy's spell with pain.
And thus her pictures plainly show,
Not nature's self but ideal glow.

And now to-day o'er canvas bent,
She strives to place these visions sent
From that bright world she loves so well,
But fancy fails to cast her spell,
And sick at heart, Gerarda sighs,
And wonders why her muse denies
The inspiration given before,
When oft in heaven her soul would soar.

But now her ear has caught a sound,
That causes heart and brain to bound,
With rapture wild, intense, sincere,
For, list! those strains are coming near;
She grasps the brush, her muse awoke,
Within those notes her genius spoke;
An Angelo might e'en be proud,
Of forms that o'er her vision crowd.

What power is this that swells that touch,
And sends it throbbing with a rush,
That renders all its hearers dumb!
If he be man, whence did he come?

Lo! 'tis the same who played with power
The wedding march that twilight hour;
The strains seem caught from souls above,
It is the very food of love.

And yet, he's neither old nor bent,
A comeliness to youth is lent;
A radiant eye, a natural grace,
An eager, noble, passionate face,—
All these are his, with genius spark,
That guides him safely through the dark,
To hearts that throb and souls that feel,
At every grand and solemn peal.

Triumphant Wagner's soul he reads,
And then with Mozart gently pleads,
And begs the weary cease to mope,
But rise and live in dreams of hope.
The sounds have ceased,—how drear life seems!
He wakes from out his land of dreams,
And finds Gerarda rapt, amazed,
In speechless ecstasy she gazed.

"Neville! thou king of heroes great,
A tale of love thou dost relate,
In tones that rend my heart in twain,
With intense agony and pain,
Forgive whate'er I say to-day,
Thy touch has ta'en my sense away;
O man that dreams, thou can'st not see,
That I, alas! doth worship thee!

"Behold! thou Orpheus, I kneel
And beg thee, if thou e'er canst feel,

13

Or sympathize with my unrest,
To thrust this dagger in my breast.
Shrink not! I can no longer live
Content in agony to writhe;
And death win thy hand given to me,
Will be one blissful ecstasy."

He starts, and lifts her from her knees,
Her features pale, and soon he sees
That tired heart so sick and sore
Can bear its grief and woe no more.
She swoons—her pulse has ceased to beat,
A holy calm, divine and sweet,
Has settled on the saintly face,
Lit up with beauty, youth and grace.

Neville amazed, in rapture stands,
Admiring hair, and face, and hands.
Forgetful then of hour and place,
He stoops to kiss the beauteous face,
And at the touch the fire of love,
So pure as to come from above,
Consumes his heart and racks his brain,
With longing fear and infinite pain.

The kiss, as with a magic spell,
Has roused Gerarda,—it seems to tell,
'Tis time to bid her conscience wake,
And off her soul this burden shake.
"Neville, forgive," with downcast eyes,
Gerarda sorrowfully cries:
"I've told thee of my love and woe,—
The things I meant thou should'st not know."

"Gerarda thou hast woke the heart,
That ne'er before felt passion's smart:
Oh! is it true thou'rt lost to me,
My love, my heart knows none but thee!"
"Enough! Neville, we must forget,
That in this hour our souls have met.
Farewell! we ne'er must meet in life,
For I'm, alas! a wedded wife."

III

Why ring those bells? what was that cry?
The night winds bear it as they sigh;
What is this crushing, maddening scene?
What do those flames of fire mean?
They surge above Gerarda's home,
Through attic, cellar, halls, they roam,
Like some terrific ghost of night,
Who longs from earth to take his flight.

Gerarda stands amid the fire,
That leaps above with mad desire,
And rings her hands in silent grief,
She fears for her there's no relief.
But now she hears a joyous shout,
A breathless silence from without,
That tells her God has heard her prayer,
And sent a noble hero there.

And here he comes, this gallant knight,
Her heart rejoices at the sight,
For 'tis Neville, with aspect grave.
Who risked his life, his love to save.
And all have perished now but she,

Her husband and her family.
Mid tears and sobs she breathes a prayer,
For loved ones who are buried there.

Neville has brushed her tears away,
Together silently they pray
And bless the Lord with thankful prayer
For all his watchfulness and care.
"Gerarda, love," he whispers now,
Implanting kisses on her brow,
"This earth will be a heaven to me,
For all my life, I'll share with thee."

First published in Eloise Bibb
Thompson's collection
Poems (1895)

The Foolish and the Wise

SALLIE RUNNER IS INTRODUCED TO SOCRATES

Mrs. Maxwell Thoro (born Audrey Lemere) tiptoed down the spacious hall toward the kitchen of her dwelling whence issued sounds, not exactly of revelry but—perhaps jubilation would be a better fit. For in a high soprano voice her colored maid-of-all-work, Sallie Runner, for the past half-hour had been informing to the accompaniment of energetic thumps of a flatiron, whomsoever it might concern that she had a robe, a crown, a harp and wings.

Mrs. Thoro moved quietly for, enjoyable as was Sallie's repertoire, one could never tell when she would do some even more enjoyable improvising, and her employer knew from long experience that Sallie's fights were much freer and more artistic when she was unaware of an audience.

Just as Mrs. Thoro reached the kitchen door the soloist started off on the verse, "I gotta shoes," so she stood quietly listening until the verse ended:

"I gotta shoes, yo' gotta shoes,
All a Gawd's chillun gotta shoes;
Wen I getto hebben goin' to put on my shoes
An' skip all ober Gawd's hebben.
Hebben, Hebben! Ever'buddy hollerin' 'bout hebben

Ain't goin' dere.

Hebben, hebben, goin' to skip all ober Gawd's hebben."

As the singer ceased she whirled around upon her employer with a loud laugh. "Ha, ha, Miss Oddry!" cried she. "I knowd yo' was dere. I sho is glad yo' done come, 'cause I'se mighty lonesome an' powerful tired. Jes' was thinkin' to myseff dat I'se goin' to try to swade Brother Runner to move away fum Starton. Nobuddy don't do nothin' here but git bornd, git married an' git daid, an' wurk, wurk, wurk! Miss Oddry, I'se goin' to tell yo' a secret."

"What is it, Sallie?" inquired Mrs. Thoro.

"I don't lak to wurk. Nuvver did."

"Why, Sallie! That is a surprise," replied her employer. "I should never have guessed it, for there is not a more capable maid in town than you are."

"Yassum, I guess dat's right. I wurks wid my might an' I does whut my hands finds to do, but taint my nature doe. Muss be my Ma's trainin' an' mazin-grace-how-sweet-de-sound mixed togedder, I reckon. Miss Oddry, does yo' know whut I'd ruther do dan anything? I'd ruther know how to read an' write dan anything in de whole, wide world, an' den I'd nuvver do nothin' else but jes' dem two."

"Well, Sallie, I'm sure you would get very tired of reading and writing all the time; but you're not too old to learn."

"Nome, not too ole, mebbe, but too dumb an' too sot in de haid, I reckun. Miss Oddry, couldn't yo' read to me or talk to me on ironin' days 'bout sumpin' outside uv Starton? Cose I wouldn't want yo' round under my feet on wash-days, but ironin'-days is fine fur lissening."

"Why yes, Sallie, I'd love to do that. Why didn't you ask me before? Mr. Thoro and I are re-reading an old school course, just for the fun of it, and I'll share it with you. I'm sure you would enjoy hearing about some of earth's greatest characters. How would you like to have me tell you about Socrates?"

"Sockertees? Huh! Funny name! Sockertees whut?"

"Well, in his time men seldom had more than one name, Sallie. He was the son of Sophroniscus and Phaenarete. He was a sculptor and a philosopher."

"Gosh!" cried Sallie. "A sculpture an' a lossipede! Wusser an' mo' uv it! But go on, Miss Oddry, tell me mo' 'bout him."

"Socrates was born about 469 years before our Lord, and died at the age of seventy. He is said to have had thick lips, a flat nose, protruding eyes, bald head, a squat figure, and a shambling gait."

"Why!" exclaimed Sallie. "He was a cullud gentmun, warn't he? Musta looked jes' lak Brudder Runner, 'cordin' to dat."

"Oh no, Sallie, he wasn't colored."

"Wal, ef he been daid all dat long time, Miss Oddry, how kin yo' tell his color?"

"Why he was an Athenian, Sallie. He lived in Greece."

"Dar now! Dat settles it! Ever'buddy knows dat my cullud folks sho do lak grease."

"Oh Sallie! 'Greece' was the name of his country, just as 'America' is the name of ours." Sallie grunted.

"Socrates," continued Mrs. Thoro, "was a very wise, just, and a good man, and he loved his country and his countrymen very much. He used to delight in wandering through the streets of Athens, conversing with those whom he met, giving them the benefit of the truths he had discovered and seeking to obtain from each more truth or new light. He spent the whole day in public, in the walks, the workshops, the gymnasiums, the porticoes, the schools and the market place at the hour it was most crowded, talking with everyone without distinction of age, sex, rank or condition. It was said that 'as he talked the hearts of all who heard him leaped up and their tears gushed out.'"

"Hole on, Miss Oddry," interrupted Sallie, "Jes' wanta ax yo' one queshun. While ole Sockertees was runnin' round the streets, shootin' off his lip an' makin' peepul cry, who was takin' keer uv his fambly? Sounds mo' an' mo' lak Brudder Runner to me."

"Well, Sallie, he had a very capable wife who bore him three sons and whose name was Xanthippe. No doubt she managed the household. The only fault Socrates found with her was that she had a violent temper."

Sallie slammed the flatiron down and braced herself against the board, arms akimbo, eyes flashing with indignation.

"Vilent temper?" cried she. "Vilent temper? Whut 'oman wouldn't had a vilent temper in a fix lak dat? I sho do symperthize wid Zantipsy an' I doesn't blame her fur gittin' tipsy needer, pore thing. I betcha she was es sweet es a angel befo' she got mahred, 'cause whut it takes to change yo' disposition, a man lak dat sho is got. It's jes' es much es a 'oman kin do to take keer uv her house right an' raise her chillun right wen her husband is doin' all he kin to hepp her, less mo' wen he ain't doin' nothin' but goin' round runnin' he mouf. Dis ain't de fust time I'se met a gentmun whut loves he kentry mo' dan he do he home folks. Go on, Miss Oddry, dear, tell me some mo' 'bout Reveral Eyesire Runner's twin brudder."

"Of course, Sallie," said Mrs. Thoro laughing, "Socrates was human and had his faults, but all in all he was a noble character."

"I hopes so, Miss Oddry, but I'll have to hear mo' fo' I 'cide."

"Socrates," resumed Mrs. Thoro, "believed in signs and omens and in following warnings received in his dreams; he also claimed that there was an inner voice which had guided him from childhood."

"Miss Oddry," expostulated Sallie, "yo' keep on tellin' me Sockertees warn't cullud, but yo' keep on tellin' me cullud things 'bout him. Wen we all b'lieve in signs an' dreams yo'-all allus says, 'It's jes' darky super-stishun an' ignunce.' How yo' splain dat?"

"Well, Sallie, in those days the most learned people were very superstitious. Of course we know better now."

"How yo' know yo' knows better, Miss Oddry? How yo' know yo' don't know wusser? Dere's one thing I done found fur sho, an' dat is dat de mo' folks knows de less dey knows. I b'lieves in dreams an' wen I follers dem I goes right. Cose I ain't nuvver heerd no cujjus voice, but ef ole Sockertees say he heerd it I b'lieve he heerd it. Nobuddy can't prove he didn't."

"Very true, Sallie, but,—"

"Jes' one minute, Miss Oddry, please. Dere's sumpin' I been thinkin' a long time, an' now I knows it. An' dat is dat wen yo' come right down to de fack-trufe uv de inside feelin's peepul is all alak; black ones is lak white ones an' dem ole ancienty ones lak Sockertees is jes' lak dese here ones right now."

"I believe there is some truth in that, Sallie, but shall I go on about Socrates?"

"Oh, yassum, Miss Oddry, I do love to hear 'bout him."

"He tried most earnestly to make people think, to reason out what was right and what wrong in their treatment of each other. He constantly repeated, 'Virtue is knowledge; Vice is ignorance', while to the young his advice was always, 'Know thyself.'"

"Humph!" interrupted Sallie. "Mighty good advice, Miss Oddry, but it's some job, b'lieve me. I'se es ole es Methusalum's billy goat now an' I ain't nuvver found myseff out yit. Dere's some new kink comin' out ev'ry day. How 'bout you, Miss Oddry?"

"I think you are right, Sallie. But don't you think we are better off if we study ourselves than if we just blunder along blindly?"

"Oh, yassum, I guess so. But how did ole Sockertees come out wid all his runnin' round an' talkin'?"

"Very sadly, I am sorry to say. Very sadly. Most of the Athenians entirely misunderstood him."

"Bound to," said Sallie.

"He made a great many unscrupulous enemies."

"Bound to," said Sallie.

"They accused him of being the very opposite of what he was."

"Bound to," said Sallie.

"And finally they tried him and condemned him to death."

Sallie set down the flatiron and folded her arms, while her eyes flew wide open in astonishment. "What?" she exclaimed. "Jes' fur talkin'? Wal I-will-be-swijjled!"

"Yes," continued Mrs. Thoro. "They imprisoned him and sent him a cup of hemlock, which is a deadly poison, to drink."

"But he had mo' gumption dan to drink it, I hope?"

"It was the law of his country, Sallie, and Socrates was always a law-abiding citizen."

"Wal, fur gosh sake!" cried Sallie. "Whut in de world was de use uv him havin' all dat tongue ef he couldn't use it to show dem peeple wherein? He mouts well been es dumd es a doodlebug!"

"But," explained Mrs. Thoro, "he had spent his whole life in trying to make the Athenians love and honor and obey their laws and he was willing to die for the same cause. He had many friends who loved him truly and they tried to persuade him to escape, but by unanswerable arguments he proved to them how wrong they were."

"Humph!" grunted Sallie. "Tonguey to de last! An' in de wrong way to de wrong ones."

"Plato, who was a friend as well as a pupil," continued Mrs. Thoro, "tells how beautifully Socrates died. He took the cup of hemlock quite calmly and cheerfully and drained it to the dregs. When his friends could not restrain their sorrow for the loss they were about to sustain, he reproved them and urged them to remember that they were about to bury, not Socrates, but the shell which had contained him, for he, himself, was about to enter the joys of the blessed. He tried to the last to make them see that unless they honored and obeyed all laws, their country could not long survive, because lawlessness was the same as suicide."

"Miss Oddry," said Sallie, solemnly, "don't yo' wisht we had one million of dem Sockertees down here in ower sunny Soufland?"

First published in the magazine
The Crisis (March 1921)

GEORGIA DOUGLAS JOHNSON

Your World

Your world is as big as you make it.
I know, for I used to abide
In the narrowest nest in a corner,
My wings pressing close to my side.

But I sighted the distant horizon
Where the skyline encircled the sea
And I throbbed with a burning desire
To travel this immensity.

I battered the cordons around me
And cradled my wings on the breeze,
Then soared to the uttermost reaches
With rapture, with power, with ease!

Uncle Rube on the Race Problem

'How'd I solve de Negro Problum?'
    Gentlemen, don't like dat wo'd!
'Mind me too much uv ol' slave times,
    When de white man wus de lo'd.

Spoutin' roun' about 'My niggahs',
    Knockin' us fum lef' to right,
Sellin' us, like we wus cattle,
    Drivin' us fum mawn till night,—

Oh, you say I'm off de subjec';
    Am a little off, I see,—
Well, de way to solve de problum,
    Is, to let de black man be.

Say, 'you fail to ketch my meanin'?'
    Now, dat's very plain to me,
Don't you know, you whites is pickin'
    On de blacks, continu'ly?

Jes' pick up de mawnin' papah,
    Anywhaur you choose to go,
When you read about de black man,
    You may bet it's somepin low.

It's all right to tell his meanness,
    Dat's, pervided it is true;
But, why, in de name uv blazes,
    Don't you tell de good things too!

No, I ain't a-cussin' either!
      Et my blood wus young an' waum,
Guess I'd sometimes, feel like cussin',
      How you whites is takin' on.

Still, I don't hol' wid dat business,
      Leave dat, fah you whites to do—
Cussin' an' a-suicidin',
      When de whole land b'longs to you.

Den, agin, ez I wus sayin',—
      Ef a black man makes a mawk,
Seems you white-folks will go crazy,
      Try'n' to keep him in de dawk.

An', ef he don't watch his cornahs,
      An' his head ain't mighty soun',
Fust he knows: some uv you white-folks
      Done reached up, an' pulled him down.

Whut you say? I'm too hawd on you?
      Whut you 'spected me to do,
When you axed me, my opinion?
      Tell you somepin' wusn't true?

Co'se dah's some exceptions 'mong you,
      An' I ain't denyin' it;
But dah's mighty few, I tell you,
      Dat kin say: 'Dis shoe don't fit.'

Yes, you say some blacks is 'on'ry;'
      So is many uv de whites;
But de black race mus' be perfec',
      'Fo' we git ou' 'equal rights.'

Foreign whites, fum ev'ry nation,
      Finds a welcome in dis lan',
Yet, dah seems to be no welcome
      Fah de native cullud man.

You don't have to 'tote his skillet,'—
      Ez de folks in Dixie say,—
Only, when you see him strugglin',
      Don't you git into his way.

Co'se, ef you is got a mind to,
      You kin lend a helpin' han',
But de best help you kin give him,
      Is, to treat him like a man.

Look at all de great improvement,
      He has made since he wus free;
Yet, de white-folks keep a-wond'ring,
      Whut's his future go'n' to be.

All time talkin' 'bout his meanness,
      An' de many things he lack,
Makin' out dey see no progress,
      Doe dey're try'n' to hol' him back.

Oh, it ain't no use in talkin',
      Ef you whites would jest play faiah,
All de wranglin' 'bout dis problum,
      Soon would vanish in de aiah.

Once dey couldn't find no method,
      Dat would put down slavery,
Till it like to split de country,
      Den, dey set de black man free.

Dat's de way wid dis race problum:
　　Ef de white-folks had a min',
Dey could fin' a answer to it,
　　Like dey did de other time.

Co'se, dah's two sides to dis problum,
　　An' dah's things de blacks should do,
But I'm talkin' 'bout you white-folks,
　　And de pawt dat b'longs to you.

'Don't know whaur to place de black man?'
　　He will fin' his place;—You'll see!
Like de foreign whites is doin',
　　When you learn to let him be.

'Den, you feah amalgamation?'
　　When de black man takes his stan',
Don't you know he'll squar' his shoulders,
　　Proud, dat he's a Af'ican?

In dis lan', to be a black man,
　　Isn't called a lucky thing;
An' dat's why some fools among us,
　　Think it smawt to mingle in.

An' you white-folks isn't blameless,
　　Some uv you is in dat too,—
Takin' ev'ry mean advantage,
　　Dat is in yo' powah to do.

But, de race will reach a station,
　　Whaur de blindes' one kin see,
Dat 'tis good to be a black man,
　　Jest ez sho', ez sho' kin be.

Den, agin, sometimes I'm thinkin',
    Dat dis 'malgamation fright's
Jes' got up by you smawt white-folks,
    Keep fum givin' us ou' rights.

Fah, ef now, in all her trials,
    Mos' uv us stick to de race,
You know well, we won't fahsake her,
    When she gits a honored place.

'Be a nation in a nation?'
    Now you're talkin' like a fool!
Whut you mean by " 'Plur'bus unyun?—"
    Many nations 'neath one rule.

Not go'n' back on dat ol' motto,
    Dat has made yo' country's name,
Jest because de race you brung here,
    Ax you fah a little claim?

Well, I 'spec' I mus' be goin',
    Gittin' kinder late, I see;
Guess nex' time 'Ol' Rube' is passin',
    Gentlemen, you'll let him be.

Oh, you say, 'you bah no malice,'
    Well, I'd ruther have it so,
But I'll hol' up fah my people,
    Whethah folks like it or no.

First published in Clara Ann
Thompson's collection *Songs
from the Wayside* (1908)

GWENDOLYN B. BENNETT

To Usward

Dedicated to all Negro Youth known and unknown who
have a song to sing, a story to tell or a vision for the
sons of earth. Especially dedicated to Jessie Fauset
upon the event of her novel, *There Is Confusion*.

Let us be still
As ginger jars are still
Upon a Chinese shelf.
And let us be contained
By entities of Self . . .
Not still with lethargy and sloth,
But quiet with the pushing of our growth.
Not self-contained with smug identity
But conscious of the strength in entity.
If any have a song to sing
That's different from the rest,
Oh let them sing
Before the urgency of Youth's behest!
For some of us have songs to sing
Of jungle heat and fires,
And some of us are solemn grown
With pitiful desires,
And there are those who feel the pull
Of seas beneath the skies,
And some there be who want to croon
Of Negro lullabies.
We claim no part with racial dearth;
We want to sing the songs of birth!
And so we stand like ginger jars

Like ginger jars bound 'round
With dust and age;
Like jars of ginger we are sealed
By nature's heritage.
But let us break the seal of years
With pungent thrusts of song,
For there is joy in long-dried tears
For whetted passions of a throng!

First published in the magazine
The Crisis (May 1924)

The Sleeper Wakes

A NOVELETTE IN THREE INSTALMENTS

Amy recognized the incident as the beginning of one of her phases. Always from a child she had been able to tell when "something was going to happen." She had been standing in Marshall's store, her young, eager gaze intent on the lovely little sample dress which was not from Paris, but quite as dainty as anything that Paris could produce. It was not the lines or even the texture that fascinated Amy so much, it was the grouping of colors—of shades. She knew the combination was just right for her.

"Let me slip it on, Miss," said the saleswoman suddenly. She had nothing to do just then, and the girl was so evidently charmed and so pretty—it was a pleasure to wait on her.

"Oh no," Amy had stammered. "I haven't time." She had already wasted two hours at the movies, and she knew at home they were waiting for her.

The saleswoman slipped the dress over the girl's pink blouse, and tucked the linen collar under so as to bring the edge of the dress next to her pretty neck. The dress was apricot-color shading into a shell pink and the shell pink shaded off again into the pearl and pink whiteness of Amy's skin. The saleswoman beamed as Amy, entranced, surveyed herself naively in the tall looking-glass.

Then it was that the incident befell. Two men walking idly through the dress-salon stopped and looked—she made an unbelievably pretty picture. One of them with a short, soft brown beard,—"fuzzy" Amy thought to herself as she caught his glance in the mirror—spoke to his companion.

"Jove, how I'd like to paint her!" But it was the look on the other man's face that caught her and thrilled her. "My God! Can't a girl be beautiful!" he said half to himself. The pair passed on.

Amy stepped out of the dress and thanked the sales-woman half absently. She wanted to get home and think, think to herself about that look. She had seen it before in men's eyes, it had been in the eyes of the men in the moving-picture which she had seen that after-noon. But she had not thought *she* could cause it. Shut up in her little room she pondered over it. Her beauty,—she was really good-looking then—she could stir people—men! A girl of seventeen has no psych-ology, she does not go beneath the surface, she accepts. But she knew she was entering on one of her phases.

She was always living in some sort of story. She had started it when as a child of five she had driven with the tall, proud, white woman to Mrs. Boldin's home. Mrs. Boldin was a bride of one year's standing then. She was slender and very, very comely, with her rich brown skin and her hair that crinkled thick and soft above a low forehead. The house was still redolent of new furniture; Mr. Boldin was spick and span—he, unlike the furniture, remained so for that matter. The white woman had told Amy that this henceforth was to be her home.

Amy was curious, fond of adventure; she did not cry. She did not, of course, realize that she was to stay here

33

indefinitely, but if she had, even at that age she would hardly have shed tears, she was always too eager, too curious to know, to taste what was going to happen next. Still since she had had almost no dealings with colored people and knew absolutely none of the class to which Mrs. Boldin belonged, she did venture one question.

"Am I going to be colored now?"

The tall white woman had flushed and paled. "You—" she began, but the words choked her. "Yes, you are going to be colored now," she ended finally. She was a proud woman, in a moment she had recovered her usual poise. Amy carried with her for many years the memory of that proud head. She never saw her again.

When she was sixteen she asked Mrs. Boldin the question which in the light of that memory had puzzled her always. "Mrs. Boldin, tell me—am I white or colored?"

And Mrs. Boldin had told her and told her truly that she did not know.

"A—a—mee!" Mrs. Boldin's voice mounted on the last syllable in a shrill crescendo. Amy rose and went downstairs.

Down in the comfortable, but rather shabby dining-room which the Boldins used after meals to sit in, Mr. Boldin, a tall black man, with aristocratic features, sat reading; little Cornelius Boldin sat practicing on a cornet, and Mrs. Boldin sat rocking. In all of their eyes was the manifestation of the light that Amy loved, but how truly she loved it, she was not to guess till years later.

"Amy," Mrs. Boldin paused in her rocking, "did you get the braid?" Of course she had not, though that was the thing she had gone to Marshall's for. Amy always forgot essentials. If she went on an errand, and she always went willingly, it was for the pure joy of going. Who knew what angels might meet one unawares? Not that Amy thought in biblical or in literary phrases. She was in the High School, it is true, but she was simply passing through, "getting by" she would have said carelessly. The only reading that had ever made any impression on her had been fairy tales read to her in those long remote days when she had lived with the tall, proud woman; and descriptions in novels or histories of beautiful, stately palaces tenanted by beautiful, stately women. She could pore over such pages for hours, her face flushed, her eyes eager.

At present she cast about for an excuse. She had so meant to get the braid. "There was a dress——" she began lamely, she was never deliberately dishonest.

Mr. Boldin cleared his throat and nervously fingered his paper. Cornelius ceased his awful playing and blinked at her shortsightedly through his thick glasses. Both of these, the man and the little boy, loved the beautiful, inconsequent creature with her airy, irresponsible ways. But Mrs. Boldin loved her too, and because she loved her she could not scold.

"Of course you forgot," she began chidingly. Then she smiled. "There was a dress that you looked at *perhaps*. But confess, didn't you go to the movies first?"

Yes, Amy confessed she had done just that. "And oh, Mrs. Boldin, it was the most wonderful picture—a girl—such a pretty one—and she was poor, awfully. And somehow she met the most wonderful people and they were so kind to her. And she married a man who was just tremendously rich and he gave her everything. I did so want Cornelius to see it."

"Huh!" said Cornelius who had been listening not

35

because he was interested, but because he wanted to call Amy's attention to his playing as soon as possible. "Huh! I don't want to look at no pretty girl. Did they have anybody looping the loop in an airship?"

"You'd better stop seeing pretty girl pictures, Amy," said Mr. Boldin kindly. "They're not always true to life. Besides, I know where you can see all the pretty girls you want without bothering to pay twenty-five cents for it."

Amy smiled at the implied compliment and went on happily studying her lessons. They were all happy in their own way. Amy because she was sure of their love and admiration, Mr. and Mrs. Boldin because of her beauty and innocence and Cornelius because he knew he had in his foster-sister a listener whom his terrible practicing could never bore. He played brokenly a piece he had found in an old music-book. "*There's an aching void in every heart, brother.*"

"Where *do* you pick up those old things, Neely?" said his mother fretfully. But Amy could not have her favorite's feelings injured.

"I think it's lovely," she announced defensively. "Cornelius, I'll ask Sadie Murray to lend me her brother's book. He's learning the cornet, too, and you can get some new pieces. Oh, isn't it awful to have to go to bed? Good-night, everybody." She smiled her charming, ever ready smile, the mere reflex of youth and beauty and content.

"You do spoil her, Mattie," said Mr. Boldin after she had left the room. "She's only seventeen—here, Cornelius, you go to bed—but it seems to me she ought to be more dependable about errands. Though she is splendid about some things," he defended her. "Look how willingly she goes off to bed. She'll be asleep before she knows it when most girls of her age would want to be in the street."

But upstairs Amy was far from sleep. She lit one gas-jet and pulled down the shades. Then she stuffed tissue paper in the keyhole and under the doors, and lit the remaining gas-jets. The light thus thrown on the mirror of the ugly oak dresser was perfect. She slipped off the pink blouse and found two scarfs, a soft yellow and a soft pink,—she had had them in a scarf-dance for a school entertainment. She wound them and draped them about her pretty shoulders and loosened her hair. In the mirror she apostrophized the beautiful, glowing vision of herself.

"There," she said, "I'm like the girl in the picture. She had nothing but her beautiful face—and she did so want to be happy." She sat down on the side of the rather lumpy bed and stretched out her arms. "I want to be happy, too." She intoned it earnestly, almost like an incantation. "I want wonderful clothes, and people around me, men adoring me, and the world before me. I want—everything! It will come, it will all come because I want it so." She sat frowning intently as she was apt to do when very much engrossed. "And we'd all be so happy. I'd give Mr. and Mrs. Boldin money! And Cornelius—he'd go to college and learn all about his old airships. Oh, if I only knew how to begin!"

Smiling, she turned off the lights and crept to bed.

II

Quite suddenly she knew she was going to run away. That was in October. By December she had accomplished her purpose. Not that she was the least bit unhappy but because she must get out in the world,—she felt caged, imprisoned. "Trenton is stifling me," she would have told you, in her unconsciously adopted "movie" diction. New York she knew was the place for her. She had her plans all made. She had sewed steadily after school for two months—as she frequently did when she wanted to buy her season's wardrobe, so besides her carfare she had $25. She went immediately to a white Y. W. C. A., stayed there two nights, found and answered an advertisement for clerk and waitress in a small confectionery and bakery-shop, was accepted and there she was launched.

Perhaps it was because of her early experience when as a tiny child she was taken from that so different home and left at Mrs. Boldin's; perhaps it was some fault in her own disposition, concentrated and egotistic as she was, but certainly she felt no pangs of separation, no fear of her future. She was cold too,—unfired though so to speak rather than icy,—and fastidious. This last quality kept her safe where morality or religion, of neither of which had she any conscious endowment, would have availed her nothing. Unbelievably then she lived two years in New York, unspoiled, untouched, going to her work on the edge of Greenwich Village early and coming back late, knowing almost no one and yet altogether happy in the expectation of something wonderful, which she knew some day must happen.

It was at the end of the second year that she met Zora Harrisson. Zora used to come into lunch with a group of habitués of the place—all of them artists and writers Amy gathered. Mrs. Harrisson (for she was married as Amy later learned) appealed to the girl because she knew so well how to afford the contrast to

38

her blonde, golden beauty. Purple, dark and regal, developed in velvets and heavy silks, and strange marine blues she wore, and thus made Amy absolutely happy. Singularly enough, the girl, intent as she was on her own life and experiences, had felt up to this time no yearning to know these strange, happy beings who surrounded her. She did miss Cornelius, but otherwise she was never lonely, or if she was she hardly knew it, for she had always lived an inner life to herself. But Mrs. Harrisson magnetized her—she could not keep her eyes from her face, from her wonderful clothes. She made conjectures about her.

The wonderful lady came in late one afternoon—an unusual thing for her. She smiled at Amy invitingly, asked some banal questions and their first conversation began. The acquaintance once struck up progressed rapidly—after a few weeks Mrs. Harrisson invited the girl to come to see her. Amy accepted quietly, unaware that anything extraordinary was happening. Zora noticed this and liked it. She had an apartment in 12th Street in a house inhabited only by artists—she was no mean one herself. Amy was fascinated by the new world into which she found herself ushered; Zora's surroundings were very beautiful and Zora herself was a study. She opened to the girl's amazed vision fields of thought and conjecture, phases of whose existence Amy, who was a builder of phases, had never dreamed. Zora had been a poor girl of good family. She had wanted to study art, she had deliberately married a rich man and as deliberately obtained in the course of four years a divorce, and she was now living in New York studying by means of her alimony and enjoying to its fullest the life she loved. She took Amy on a footing with herself—the girl's refinement, her beauty, her interest in colors

39

(though this in Amy at that time was purely sporadic, never consciously encouraged), all this gave Zora a figure about which to plan and build a romance. Amy had told her the truth, but not all about her coming to New York. She had grown tired of Trenton—her people were all dead—the folks with whom she lived were kind and good but not "inspiring" (she had borrowed the term from Zora and it was true, the Boldins, when one came to think of it, were not "inspiring"), so she had run away.

Zora had gone into raptures. "What an adventure! My dear, the world is yours. Why, with your looks and your birth, for I suppose you really belong to the Kildares who used to live in Philadelphia, I think there was a son who ran off and married an actress or someone— they disowned him I remember,—you can reach any height. You must marry a wealthy man—perhaps someone who is interested in art and who will let you pursue your studies." She insisted always that Amy had run away in order to study art. "But luck like that comes to few," she sighed, remembering her own plight, for Mr. Harrisson had been decidedly unwilling to let her pursue her studies, at least to the extent she wished. "Anyway you must marry wealth,—one can always get a divorce," she ended sagely.

Amy—she came to Zora's every night now—used to listen dazedly at first. She had accepted willingly enough Zora's conjecture about her birth, came to believe it in fact—but she drew back somewhat at such wholesale exploitation of people to suit one's own convenience, still she did not probe too far into this thought—nor did she grasp at all the infamy of exploitation of self. She ventured one or two objections, however, but Zora brushed everything aside.

"Everybody is looking out for himself," she said airily. "I am interested in you, for instance, not for philanthropy's sake, but because I am lonely, and you are charming and pretty and don't get tired of hearing me talk. You'd better come and live with me awhile, my dear, six months or a year. It doesn't cost any more for two than for one, and you can always leave when we get tired of each other. A girl like you can always get a job. If you are worried about being dependent you can pose for me and design my frocks, and oversee Julienne"—her maid-of-all-work—"I'm sure she's a stupendous robber."

Amy came, not at all overwhelmed by the good luck of it—good luck was around the corner more or less for everyone, she supposed. Moreover, she was beginning to absorb some of Zora's doctrine—she, too, must look out for herself. Zora *was* lonely, she *did* need companionship; Julienne *was* careless about change and odd blouses and left-over dainties. Amy had her own sense of honor. She carried out faithfully her share of the bargain, cut down waste, renovated Zora's clothes, posed for her, listened to her endlessly and bore with her fitfulness. Zora was truly grateful for this last. She was temperamental but Amy had good nerves and her strong natural inclination to let people do as they wanted stood her in good stead. She was a little stolid, a little unfeeling under her lovely exterior. Her looks at this time belied her—her perfect ivory-pink face, her deep luminous eyes,—very brown they were with purple depths that made one think of pansies—her charming, rather wide mouth, her whole face set in a frame of very soft, very live, brown hair which grew in wisps and tendrils and curls and waves back from her smooth, young forehead. All this made one look for softness and ingenuousness. The ingenuousness was there, but not the softness—except of her fresh, vibrant loveliness.

On the whole then she progressed famously with Zora. Sometimes the latter's callousness shocked her, as when they would go strolling through the streets south of Washington Square. The children, the people all foreign, all dirty, often very artistic, always immensely human, disgusted Zora except for "local color"—she really could reproduce them wonderfully. But she almost hated them for being what they were.

"Br-r-r, dirty little brats!" she would say to Amy. "Don't let them touch me." She was frequently amazed at her protégée's utter indifference to their appearance, for Amy herself was the pink of daintiness. They were turning from MacDougall into Bleecker Street one day and Amy had patted a child—dirty, but lovely—on the head.

"They are all people just like anybody else, just like you and me, Zora," she said in answer to her friend's protest.

"You *are* the true democrat," Zora returned with a shrug. But Amy did not understand her.

Not the least of Amy's services was to come between Zora and the too pressing attention of the men who thronged about her.

"Oh, go and talk to Amy," Zora would say, standing slim and gorgeous in some wonderful evening gown. She was an extraordinarily attractive creature, very white and pink, with great ropes of dazzling gold hair, and that look of no-age which only American women possess. As a matter of fact she was thirty-nine, immensely sophisticated and selfish, even, Amy thought, a little cruel. Her present mode of living just suited her; she could not stand any condition that bound her, anything

42

at all *exigeant*. It was useless for anyone to try to influence her. If she did not want to talk, she would not.

The men used to obey her orders and seek Amy sulkily at first, but afterwards with considerably more interest. She was so lovely to look at. But they really, as Zora knew, preferred to talk to the older woman, for while with Zora indifference was a rôle—with Amy it was natural and she was also a trifle shallow. She had the admiration she craved, she was comfortable, she asked no more. Moreover she thought the men, with the exception of Stuart James Wynne, rather uninteresting—they were faddists for the most part, crazy not about art or music, but merely about some phase such as cubism or syncopation.

Wynne, who was much older than the other half-dozen men who weekly paid Zora homage—impressed her by his suggestion of power. He was a retired broker, immensely wealthy (Zora, who had known him since childhood, informed her), very set and purposeful and very polished. He was perhaps fifty-five, widely traveled, of medium height, very white skin and clear, frosty, blue eyes, with sharp, proud features. He liked Amy from the beginning, her childishness touched him. In particular he admired her pliability—not knowing it was really indifference. He had been married twice; one wife had divorced him, the other had died. Both marriages were unsuccessful owing to his dominant, rather unsympathetic nature. But he had softened considerably with years, though he still had decided views, was glad to see that Amy, in spite of Zora's influence, neither smoked nor drank. He liked her shallowness—she fascinated him.

Zora had told him much—just the kind of romantic story to appeal to the rich, powerful man. Here was beauty forlorn, penniless, of splendid birth,—for Zora once having connected Amy with the Philadelphia Kildares never swerved from that belief. Amy seemed to Wynne everything a girl should be—she was so unspoiled, so untouched. He asked her to marry him. If she had tried she could not have acted more perfectly. She looked at him with her wonderful eyes.

"But I am poor, ignorant—a nobody," she stammered. "I'm afraid I don't love you either," she went on in her pretty troubled voice, "though I do like you very, very much."

He liked her honesty and her self-depreciation, even her coldness. The fact that she was not flattered seemed to him an extra proof of her native superiority. He, himself, was a representative of one of the South's oldest families, though he had lived abroad lately.

"I have money and influence," he told her gravely, "but I count them nothing without you." And as for love—he would teach her that, he ended, his voice shaking a little. Underneath all his chilly, polished exterior he really cared.

"It seems an unworthy thing to say," he told her wistfully, for she seemed very young beside his experienced fifty-five years, "but anything you wanted in this world could be yours. I could give it to you,—clothes, houses and jewels."

"Don't be an idiot," Zora had said when Amy told her. "Of course, marry him. He'll give you a beautiful home and position. He's probably no harder to get along with than anybody else, and if he is, there is always the divorce court."

It seemed to Amy somehow that she was driving a bargain—how infamous a one she could not suspect. But Zora's teachings had sunk deep. Wynne loved her,

44

and he could secure for her what she wanted. "And after all," she said to herself once, "it really is my dream coming true."

She resolved to marry him. There were two weeks of delirious, blissful shopping. Zora was very generous. It seemed to Amy that the whole world was contributing largesse to her happiness. She was to have just what she wanted and as her taste was perfect she afforded almost as much pleasure to the people from whom she bought as to herself. In particular she brought rapture to an exclusive modiste in Forty-second Street who exclaimed at her "so perfect taste".

"Mademoiselle is of a marvellous, of an absolute correctness," she said.

Everything whirled by. After the shopping there was the small, impressive wedding. Amy stumbled somehow through the service, struck by its awful solemnity. Then later there was the journey and the big house waiting them in the small town, fifty miles south of Richmond. Wynne was originally from Georgia, but business and social interests had made it necessary for him to be nearer Washington and New York.

Amy was absolute mistress of himself and his home, he said, his voice losing its coldness. "Ah, my dear, you'll never realize what you mean to me—I don't envy any other man in the world. You are so beautiful, so sweet, so different!"

III

From the very beginning *he* was different from what she had supposed. To start with he was far, far wealthier, and he had, too, a tradition, a family-pride which to

45

Amy was inexplicable. Still more inexplicably he had a race-pride. To his wife this was not only strange but foolish. She was as Zora had once suggested, the true democrat. Not that she preferred the company of her maids, though the reason for this did not lie *per se* in the fact that they were maids. There was simply no common ground. But she was uniformly kind, a trait which had she been older would have irritated her husband. As it was, he saw in it only an additional indication of her freshness, her lack of worldliness which seemed to him the attributes of an inherent refinement and goodness untouched by experience.

He, himself, was intolerant of all people of inferior birth or standing and looked with contempt on foreigners, except the French and English. All the rest were variously "guineys", "niggers", and "wops", and all of them he genuinely despised and hated, and talked of them with the huge intolerant carelessness characteristic of occidental civilization. Amy was never able to understand it. People were always first and last, just people to her. Growing up as the average colored American girl does grow up, surrounded by types of every hue, color and facial configuration she had had no absolute ideal. She was not even aware that there was one. Wynne, who in his grim way had a keen sense of humor, used to be vastly amused at the artlessness with which she let him know that she did not consider him good-looking. She never wanted him to wear anything but dark blue, or sombre mixtures always.

"They take away from that awful whiteness of your skin," she used to tell him, "and deepen the blue of your eyes."

In the main she made no attempt to understand him, as indeed she made no attempt to understand anything.

The result, of course, was that such ideas as seeped into her mind stayed there, took growth and later bore fruit. But just at this period she was like a well-cared for, sleek, house-pet, delicately nurtured, velvety, content to let her days pass by. She thought almost nothing of her art just now, except as her sensibilities were jarred by an occasional disharmony. Likewise, even to herself, she never criticized Wynne, except when some act or attitude of his stung. She could never understand why he, so fastidious, so versed in elegance of word and speech, so careful in his surroundings, even down to the last detail of glass and napery, should take such evident pleasure in literature of a certain prurient type. He fairly revelled in the realistic novels which to her depicted sheer badness. He would get her to read to him, partly because he liked to be read to, mostly because he enjoyed the realism and in a slighter degree because he enjoyed seeing her shocked. Her point of view amused him.

"What funny people," she would say naively, "to do such things." She could not understand the liaisons and intrigues of women in the society novels, such infamy was stupid and silly. If one starved, it was conceivable that one might steal; if one were intentionally injured, one might hit back, even murder; but deliberate nastiness she could not envisage. The stories, after she had read them to him, passed out of her mind as completely as though they had never existed.

Picture the two of them spending three years together with practically no friction. To his dominance and intolerance she opposed a soft and unobtrusive indifference. What she wanted she had, ease, wealth, adoration, love, too, passionate and imperious, but she had never known any other kind. She was growing cleverer also, her knowledge of French was increasing, she was acquiring a knowledge of politics, of commerce and of the big social questions, for Wynne's interests were exhaustive and she did most of his reading for him. Another woman might have yearned for a more youthful companion, but her native coldness kept her content. She did not love him, she had never really loved anybody, but little Cornelius Boldin—he had been such an enchanting, such a darling baby, she remembered,—her heart contracted painfully when she thought as she did very often of his warm softness.

"He must be a big boy now," she would think almost maternally, wondering—once she had been so sure!—if she would ever see him again. But she was very fond of Wynne, and he was crazy over her just as Zora had predicted. He loaded her with gifts, dresses, flowers, jewels—she amused him because none but colored stones appealed to her.

"Diamonds are so hard, so cold, and pearls are dead," she told him.

Nothing ever came between them, but his ugliness, his hatefulness to dependents. It hurt her so, for she was naturally kind in her careless, uncomprehending way. True, she had left Mrs. Boldin without a word, but she did not guess how completely Mrs. Boldin loved her. She would have been aghast had she realized how stricken her flight had left them. At twenty-two, Amy was still as good, as unspoiled, as pure as a child. Of course with all this she was too unquestioning, too self-ish, too vain, but they were all faults of her lovely, lovely flesh. Wynne's intolerance finally got on her nerves. She used to blush for his unkindness. All the servants were colored, but she had long since ceased to think that perhaps she, too, was colored, except when he, by insult

48

toward an employee, overt always at least implied, made her realize his contemptuous dislike and disregard for a dark skin or Negro blood.

"Stuart, how can you say such things?" she would expostulate. "You can't expect a man to stand such language as that." And Wynne would sneer, "A man—you don't consider a nigger a man, do you? Oh, Amy, don't be such a fool. You've got to keep them in their places."

Some innate sense of the fitness of things kept her from condoling outspokenly with the servants, but they knew she was ashamed of her husband's ways. Of course, they left—it seemed to Amy that Peter, the butler, was always getting new "help",—but most of the upper servants stayed, for Wynne paid handsomely and although his orders were meticulous and insistent, the retinue of employees was so large that the individual's work was light.

Most of the servants who did stay on in spite of Wynne's occasional insults had a purpose in view. Callie, the cook, Amy found out, had two children at Howard University—of course she never came in contact with Wynne—the chauffeur had a crippled sister. Rose, Amy's maid and purveyor of much outside information, was the chief support of her family. About Peter, Amy knew nothing; he was a striking, taciturn man, very competent, who had left the Wynnes' service years before and had returned in Amy's third year. Wynne treated him with comparative respect. But Stephen, the new valet, met with entirely different treatment. Amy's heart yearned toward him, he was like Cornelius, with shortsighted, patient eyes, always willing, a little over-eager. Amy recognized him for what he was; a boy of respectable, ambitious parentage, striving for the means for an education; naturally far above his

49

present calling, yet willing to pass through all this as a means to an end. She questioned Rosa about him.

"Oh, Stephen," Rosa told her, "yes'm, he's workin' for fair. He's got a brother at the Howard's and a sister at Smith's. Yes'm, it do seem a little hard on him, but Stephen, he say, they're both goin' to turn roun' and help him when they get through. That blue silk has a rip in it, Miss Amy, if you was thinkin' of wearin' that. Yes'm, somehow I don't think Steve's very strong, kinda worries like. I guess he's sorta nervous."

Amy told Wynne. "He's such a nice boy, Stuart," she pleaded, "it hurts me to have you so cross with him. Anyway don't call him names." She was both surprised and frightened at the feeling in her that prompted her to interfere. She had held so aloof from other people's interests all these years.

"I *am* colored," she told herself that night. "I feel it inside of me. I must be or I couldn't care so about Stephen. Poor boy, I suppose Cornelius is just like him. I wish Stuart would let him alone. I wonder if all white people are like that. Zora was hard, too, on unfortunate people." She pondered over it a bit. "I wonder what Stuart would say if he knew I was colored?" She lay perfectly still, her smooth brow knitted, thinking hard. "But he loves me," she said to herself still silently. "He'll always love my looks," and she fell to thinking that all the wonderful happenings in her sheltered, pampered life had come to her through her beauty. She reached out an exquisite arm, switched on a light, and picking up a hand-mirror from a dressing-table, fell to studying her face. She was right. It was her chiefest asset. She forgot Stephen and fell asleep.

But in the morning her husband's voice issuing from his dressing-room across the hall, awakened her. She listened drowsily. Stephen, leaving the house the day before, had been met by a boy with a telegram. He had taken it, slipped it into his pocket, (he was just going to the mail-box) and had forgotten to deliver it until now, nearly twenty-four hours later. She could hear Stuart's storm of abuse—it was terrible, made up as it was of oaths and insults to the boy's ancestry. There was a moment's lull. Then she heard him again.

"If your brains are a fair sample of that black wench of a sister of yours——"

She sprang up then thrusting her arms as she ran into her pink dressing-gown. She got there just in time. Stephen, his face quivering, was standing looking straight into Wynne's smoldering eyes. In spite of herself, Amy was glad to see the boy's bearing. But he did not notice her.

"You devil!" he was saying. "You white-faced devil! I'll make you pay for that!" He raised his arm. Wynne did not blench.

With a scream she was between them. "Go, Stephen, go,—get out of the house. Where do you think you are? Don't you know you'll be hanged, lynched, tortured?" Her voice shrilled at him.

Wynne tried to thrust aside her arms that clung and twisted. But she held fast till the door slammed behind the fleeing boy.

"God, let me by, Amy!" As suddenly as she had clasped him she let him go, ran to the door, fastened it and threw the key out the window.

He took her by the arm and shook her. "Are you mad? Didn't you hear him threaten me, me,—a nigger threaten me?" His voice broke with anger, "And you're letting him get away! Why, I'll get him. I'll set blood-hounds on him, I'll have every white man in this town after him! He'll be hanging so high by midnight—" he made for the other door, cursing, half insane.

How, *how* could she keep him back! She hated her weak arms with their futile beauty! She sprang toward him. "Stuart, wait," she was breathless and sobbing. She said the first thing that came into her head. "Wait, Stuart, you cannot do this thing." She thought of Cornelius—suppose it had been he—"Stephen,—that boy,—he is my brother."

He turned on her. "What!" he said fiercely, then laughed a short laugh of disdain. "You are crazy," he said roughly, "My God, Amy! How can you even in jest associate yourself with these people? Don't you suppose I know a white girl when I see one? There's no use in telling a lie like that."

Well, there was no help for it. There was only one way. He had turned back for a moment, but she must keep him many moments—an hour. Stephen must get out of town.

She caught his arm again. "Yes," she told him, "I did lie. Stephen is not my brother, I never saw him before." The light of relief that crept into his eyes did not escape her, it only nerved her. "But I *am* colored," she ended.

Before he could stop her she had told him all about the tall white woman. "She took me to Mrs. Boldin's and gave me to her to keep. She would never have taken me to her if I had been white. If you lynch this boy, I'll let the world, your world, know that your wife is a colored woman."

He sat down like a man suddenly stricken old, his face ashen. "Tell me about it again," he commanded. And she obeyed, going mercilessly into every damning detail.

Amazingly her beauty availed her nothing. If she had been an older woman, if she had had Zora's age and experience, she would have been able to gauge exactly her influence over Wynne. Though even then in similar circumstances she would have taken the risk and acted in just the same manner. But she was a little bewildered at her utter miscalculation. She had thought he might not want his friends—his world by which he set such store—to know that she was colored, but she had not dreamed it could make any real difference to him. He had chosen her, poor and ignorant, out of a host of women, and had told her countless times of his love. To herself Amy Wynne was in comparison with Zora for instance, stupid and uninteresting. But his constant, unsolicited iterations had made her accept his idea.

She was just the same woman she told herself, she had not changed, she was still beautiful, still charming, still "different". Perhaps that very difference had its being in the fact of her mixed blood. She had been his wife—there were memories—she could not see how he could give her up. The suddenness of the divorce carried her off her feet. Dazedly she left him—though almost without a pang for she had only liked him. She had been perfectly honest about this, and he, although consumed by the fierceness of his emotion toward her, had gradually forced himself to be content, for at least she had never made him jealous.

She was to live in a small house of his in New York, up town in the 80's. Peter was in charge and there were a new maid and a cook. The servants, of course, knew of the separation, but nobody guessed why. She was living on a much smaller basis than the one to which she had become so accustomed in the last three years. But she was very comfortable. She felt, at any rate she manifested, no qualms at receiving alimony from Wynne. That was the way things happened, she supposed when she thought of it at all. Moreover, it seemed to her perfectly in keeping with Wynne's former attitude toward her; she did not see how he could do less. She expected people to be consistent. That was why she was so amazed that he in spite of his oft iterated love, could let her go. If she had felt half the love for him which he had professed for her, she would not have sent him away if he had been a leper.

"Why I'd stay with him," she told herself, "if he were one, even as I feel now."

She was lonely in New York. Perhaps it was the first time in her life that she had felt so. Zora had gone to Paris the first year of her marriage and had not come back.

The days dragged on emptily. One thing helped her. She had gone one day to the modiste from whom she had bought her trousseau. The woman remembered her perfectly—"The lady with the exquisite taste for colors—ah, madame, but you have the rare gift." Amy was grateful to be taken out of her thoughts. She bought one or two daring but altogether lovely creations and let fall a few suggestions:

"That brown frock, Madame,—you say it has been on your hands a long time? Yes? But no wonder. See, instead of that dead white you should have a shade of ivory, that white cheapens it." Deftly she caught up a bit of ivory satin and worked out her idea. Madame was ravished.

"But yes, Madame Ween is correct,—as always. Oh,

what a pity that the Madame is so wealthy. If she were only a poor girl—Mlle. Antoine with the best eye for color in the place has just left, gone back to France to nurse her brother—this World War is of such a horror! If someone like Madame, now, could be found, to take the little Antoine's place!"

Some obscure impulse drove Amy to accept the half proposal: "Oh! I don't know, I have nothing to do just now. My husband is abroad." Wynne had left her with that impression. "I could contribute the money to the Red Cross or to charity."

The work was the best thing in the world for her. It kept her from becoming too introspective, though even then she did more serious, connected thinking than she had done in all the years of her varied life.

She missed Wynne definitely, chiefly as a guiding influence for she had rarely planned even her own amusements. Her dependence on him had been absolute. She used to picture him to herself as he was before the trouble—and his changing expressions as he looked at her, of amusement, interest, pride, a certain little teasing quality that used to come into his eyes, which always made her adopt her "spoiled child air", as he used to call it. It was the way he liked her best. Then last, there was that look he had given her the morning she had told him she was colored—it had depicted so many emotions, various and yet distinct. There were dismay, disbelief, coldness, a final aloofness.

There was another expression, too, that she thought of sometimes—the look on the face of Mr. Packard, Wynne's lawyer. She, herself, had attempted no defense.

"For God's sake why did you tell him, Mrs. Wynne?" Packard asked her. His curiosity got the better of him.

"You couldn't have been in love with that yellow rascal," he blurted out. "She's too cold really, to love anybody," he told himself. "If you didn't care about the boy why should you have told?"

She defended herself feebly. "He looked so like little Cornelius Boldin," she replied vaguely, "and he couldn't help being colored." A clerk came in then and Packard said no more. But into his eyes had crept a certain reluctant respect. She remembered the look, but could not define it.

She was so sorry about the trouble now, she wished it had never happened. Still if she had it to repeat she would act in the same way again. "There was nothing else for me to do," she used to tell herself.

But she missed Wynne unbelievably.

If it had not been for Peter, her life would have been almost that of a nun. But Peter, who read the papers and kept abreast of the times, constantly called her attention, with all due respect, to the meetings, the plays, the sights which she ought to attend or see. She was truly grateful to him. She was very kind to all three of the servants. They had the easiest "places" in New York, the maids used to tell their friends. As she never entertained, and frequently dined out, they had a great deal of time off.

She had been separated from Wynne for ten months before she began to make any definite plans for her future. Of course, she could not go on like this always. It came to her suddenly that probably she would go to Paris and live there—why or how she did not know. Only Zora was there and lately she had begun to think that her life was to be like Zora's. They had been amazingly parallel up to this time. Of course she would have to wait until after the war.

She sat musing about it one day in the big sitting-room which she had had fitted over into a luxurious studio. There was a sewing-room off to the side from which Peter used to wheel into the room waxen figures of all colorings and contours so that she could drape the various fabrics about them to be sure of the best results. But today she was working out a scheme for one of Madame's customers, who was of her own color and size and she was her own lay-figure. She sat in front of the huge pier glass, a wonderful soft yellow silk draped about her radiant loveliness.

"I could do some serious work in Paris," she said half aloud to herself. "I suppose if I really wanted to, I could be very successful along this line."

Somewhere downstairs an electric bell buzzed, at first softly, then after a slight pause, louder, and more insistently.

"If Madame sends me that lace today," she was thinking, idly, "I could finish this and start on the pink. I wonder why Peter doesn't answer the bell."

She remembered then that Peter had gone to New Rochelle on business and she had sent Ellen to Altman's to find a certain rare velvet and had allowed Mary to go with her. She would dine out, she told them, so they need not hurry. Evidently she was alone in the house.

Well she could answer the bell. She had done it often enough in the old days at Mrs. Boldin's. Of course it was the lace. She smiled a bit as she went down stairs thinking how surprised the delivery-boy would be to see her arrayed thus early in the afternoon. She hoped he wouldn't go. She could see him through the long, thick panels of glass in the vestibule and front door. He was just turning about as she opened the door.

57

This was no delivery-boy, this man whose gaze fell on her hungry and avid. This was Wynne. She stood for a second leaning against the door-jamb, a strange figure surely in the sharp November weather. Some leaves—brown, skeleton shapes—rose and swirled unnoticed about her head. A passing letter-carrier looked at them curiously.

"What are you doing answering the door?" Wynne asked her roughly. "Where is Peter? Go in, you'll catch cold."

She was glad to see him. She took him into the drawing-room—a wonderful study in browns—and looked at him and looked at him.

"Well," he asked her, his voice eager in spite of the commonplace words, "are you glad to see me? Tell me what do you do with yourself."

She could not talk fast enough, her eyes clinging to his face. Once it struck her that he had changed in some indefinable way. Was it a slight coarsening of that refined aristocratic aspect? Even in her subconsciousness she denied it.

He had come back to her.

"So I design for Madame when I feel like it, and send the money to the Red Cross and wonder when you are coming back to me." For the first time in their acquaintanceship she was conscious deliberately of trying to attract, to hold him. She put on her spoiled child air which had once been so successful.

"It took you long enough to get here," she pouted. She was certain of him now. His mere presence assured her.

They sat silent a moment, the late November sun bathing her head in an austere glow of chilly gold. As she sat there in the big brown chair she was, in her

58

yellow dress, like some mysterious emanation, some wraith-like aura developed from the tone of her surroundings.

He rose and came toward her, still silent. She grew nervous, and talked incessantly with sudden unusual gestures. "Oh, Stuart, let me give you tea. It's right there in the pantry off the dining-room. I can wheel the table in." She rose, a lovely creature in her yellow robe. He watched her intently.

"Wait," he bade her.

She paused almost on tiptoe, a dainty golden butterfly.

"You are coming back to live with me?" he asked her hoarsely.

For the first time in her life she loved him.

"Of course I am coming back," she told him softly. "Aren't you glad? Haven't you missed me? I didn't see how you *could* stay away. Oh! Stuart, what a wonderful ring!"

For he had slipped on her finger a heavy dull gold band, with an immense sapphire in an oval setting—a beautiful thing of Italian workmanship.

"It is so like you to remember," she told him gratefully. "I love colored stones." She admired it, turning it around and around on her slender finger.

How silent he was, standing there watching her with his sombre yet eager gaze. It made her troubled, uneasy. She cast about for something to say.

"You can't think how I've improved since I saw you, Stuart. I've read all sorts of books—Oh! I'm learned," she smiled at him. "And Stuart," she went a little closer to him, twisting the button on his perfect coat, "I'm so sorry about it all,—about Stephen, that boy you know. I just couldn't help interfering. But when we're married

59

again, if you'll just remember how it hurts me to have you so cross—"

He interrupted her. "I wasn't aware that I spoke of our marrying again," he told her, his voice steady, his blue eyes cold.

She thought he was teasing. "Why you just asked me to. You said 'aren't you coming back to live with me—'"

"Yes," he acquiesced, "I said just that—'to live with me'."

Still she didn't comprehend. "But what do you mean?" she asked bewildered.

"What do you suppose a man means," he returned deliberately, "when he asks a woman to live with him, but not to marry him?"

She sat down heavily in the brown chair, all glowing ivory and yellow against its sombre depths.

"Like the women in those awful novels?" she whispered. "Not like those women!—Oh Stuart! you don't mean it!" Her very heart was numb.

"But you must care a little—" she was amazed at her own depth of feeling. "Why I care—there are all those memories back of us—you must want me really—"

"I do want you", he told her tensely. "I want you damnably. But—well—I might as well out with it—A white man like me simply doesn't marry a colored woman. After all what difference need it make to you? We'll live abroad—you'll travel, have all the things you love. Many a white woman would envy you." He stretched out an eager hand.

She evaded it, holding herself aloof as though his touch were contaminating. Her movement angered him.

Like a rending veil suddenly the veneer of his high polish cracked and the man stood revealed.

60

"Oh, hell!" he snarled at her roughly. "Why don't you stop posing? What do you think you are anyway? Do you suppose I'd take you for my wife—what do you think can happen to you? What man of your own race could give you what you want? You don't suppose I am going to support you this way forever, do you? The court imposed no alimony. You've got to come to it sooner or later—you're bound to fall to some white man. What's the matter—I'm not rich enough?"

Her face flamed at that—"As though it were *that* that mattered!"

He gave her a deadly look. "Well, isn't it? Ah, my girl, you forget you told me you didn't love me when you married me. You sold yourself to me then. Haven't I reason to suppose you are waiting for a higher bidder?"

At these words something in her died forever, her youth, her illusions, her happy, happy blindness. She saw life leering mercilessly in her face. It seemed to her that she would give all her future to stamp out, to kill the contempt in his frosty insolent eyes. In a sudden rush of savagery she struck him, struck him across his hateful sneering mouth with the hand which wore his ring.

As *she* fell, reeling under the fearful impact of his brutal but involuntary blow, her mind caught at, registered two things. A little thin stream of blood was trickling across his chin. She had cut him with the ring, she realized with a certain savage satisfaction. And there was something else which she must remember, which she *would* remember if only she could fight her way out of this dreadful clinging blackness, which was bearing down upon her—closing her in.

When she came to she sat up holding her bruised, aching head in her palms, trying to recall what it was that had impressed her so.

Oh, yes, her very mind ached with the realization. She lay back again on the floor, prone, anything to relieve that intolerable pain. But her memory, her thoughts went on.

"Nigger," he had called her as she fell, "nigger, nigger," and again, "nigger."

"He despised me absolutely," she said to herself wonderingly, "because I was colored. And yet he wanted me."

V

Somehow she reached her room. Long after the servants had come in, she lay face downward across her bed, thinking. How she hated Wynne, how she hated herself! And for ten months she had been living off his money although in no way had she a claim on him. Her whole body burned with the shame of it.

In the morning she rang for Peter. She faced him, white and haggard, but if the man noticed her condition, he made no sign. He was, if possible, more imperturbable than ever.

"Peter," she told him, her eyes and voice very steady, "I am leaving this house today and shall never come back."

"Yes, Miss."

"I shall want you to see to the packing and storing of the goods and to send the keys and the receipts for the jewelry and valuables to Mr. Packard in Baltimore."

"Yes, Miss."

"And, Peter, I am very poor now and shall have no money besides what I can make for myself."

"Yes, Miss."

Would nothing surprise him, she wondered dully.

She went on, "I don't know whether you knew it or not, Peter, but I am colored, and hereafter I mean to live among my own people. Do you think you could find me a little house or a little cottage not too far from New York?"

He had a little place in New Rochelle, he told her, his manner altering not one whit, or better yet his sister had a four-room house in Orange, with a garden, if he remembered correctly. Yes, he was sure there was a garden. It would be just the thing for Mrs. Wynne.

She had four hundred dollars of her very own which she had earned by designing for Madame. She paid the maids a month in advance—they were to stay as long as Peter needed them. She, herself, went to a small hotel in Twenty-eighth Street, and here Peter came for her at the end of ten days, with the acknowledgement of the keys and receipts from Mr. Packard. Then he accompanied her to Orange and installed her in her new home.

"I wish I could afford to keep you, Peter," she said a little wistfully, "but I am very poor. I am heavily in debt and I must get that off my shoulders at once."

Mrs. Wynne was very kind, he was sure; he could think of no one with whom he would prefer to work. Furthermore, he often ran down from New Rochelle to see his sister; he would come in from time to time, and in the spring would plant the garden if she wished.

She hated to see him go, but she did not dwell long on that. Her only thought was to work and work and work and save until she could pay Wynne back. She had not lived very extravagantly during those ten months and Peter was a perfect manager—in spite of her remonstrances he had given her every month an account of his expenses. She had made arrangements with Madame to be her regular designer. The French woman guessing that more than whim was behind this move drove a very shrewd bargain, but even then the pay was excellent. With care, she told herself, she could be free within two years, three at most.

She lived a dull enough existence now, going to work steadily every morning and getting home late at night. Almost it was like those early days when she had first left Mrs. Boldin, except that now she had no high sense of adventure, no expectation of great things to come, which might buoy her up. She no longer thought of phases and the proper setting for her beauty. Once indeed catching sight of her face late one night in the mirror in her tiny work-room in Orange, she stopped and scanned herself, loathing what she saw there.

"You *thing*!" she said to the image in the glass, "if you hadn't been so vain, so shallow!" And she had struck herself violently again and again across the face until her head ached.

But such fits of passion were rare. She had a curious sense of freedom in these days, a feeling that at last her brain, her senses were liberated from some hateful clinging thralldom. Her thoughts were always busy. She used to go over that last scene with Wynne again and again trying to probe the inscrutable mystery which she felt was at the bottom of the affair. She groped her way toward a solution, but always something stopped her. Her impulse to strike, she realized, and his brutal rejoinder had been actuated by something more than mere sex antagonism, there was *race* antagonism there—two elements clashing. That much she could fathom. But that he despising her, hating her for not being white should yet desire her! It seemed to her that his attitude toward her—hate and yet desire, was the attitude in microcosm of the whole white world toward her own, toward that world to which those few possible strains of black blood so tenuously and yet so tenaciously linked her.

Once she got hold of a big thought. Perhaps there *was* some root, some racial distinction woven in with the stuff of which she was formed which made her persistently kind and unexacting. And perhaps in the same way this difference, helplessly, inevitably operated in making Wynne and his kind, cruel or at best indifferent. Her reading for Wynne reacted to her thought—she remembered the grating insolence of white exploiters in foreign lands, the wrecking of African villages, the destruction of homes in Tasmania. She couldn't imagine where Tasmania was, but wherever it was, it had been the realest thing in the world to its crude inhabitants.

Gradually she reached a decision. There were two divisions of people in the world—on the one hand insatiable desire for power; keenness, mentality; a vast and cruel pride. On the other there was ambition, it is true, but modified, a certain humble sweetness, too much inclination to trust, an unthinking, unswerving loyalty. All the advantages in the world accrued to the first division. But without bitterness she chose the second. She wanted to be colored, she hoped she was colored. She wished even that she did not have to take advantage of her appearance to earn her living. But that was to meet an end. After all she had contracted her debt with a white man, she would pay him with a white man's money.

The years slipped by—four of them. One day a letter came from Mr. Packard. Mrs. Wynne had sent him the last penny of the sum received from Mr. Wynne from

February to November, 1914. Mr. Wynne had refused to touch the money, it was and would be indefinitely at Mrs. Wynne's disposal.

She never even answered the letter. Instead she dismissed the whole incident,—Wynne and all,—from her mind and began to plan for her future. She was free, free! She had paid back her sorry debt with labor, money and anguish. From now on she could do as she pleased. Almost she caught herself saying "something is going to happen." But she checked herself, she hated her old attitude.

But something *was* happening. Insensibly from the moment she knew of her deliverance, her thoughts turned back to a stifled hidden longing, which had lain, it seemed to her, an eternity in her heart. Those days with Mrs. Boldin! At night,—on her way to New York,—in the work-rooms,—her mind was busy with little intimate pictures of that happy, wholesome, unpretentious life. She could see Mrs. Boldin, clean and portly, in a lilac chambray dress, upbraiding her for some trifling, yet exasperating fault. And Mr. Boldin, immaculate and slender, with his noticeably polished air—how kind he had always been, she remembered. And lastly, Cornelius; Cornelius in a thousand attitudes and engaged in a thousand occupations, brown and near-sighted and sweet—devoted to his pretty sister, as he used to call her; Cornelius, who used to come to her as a baby as willingly as to his mother; Cornelius spelling out colored letters on his blocks, pointing to them stickily with a brown, perfect finger; Cornelius singing like an angel in his breathy, sexless voice and later murdering everything possible on his terrible cornet. How had she ever been able to leave them all and the dear shabbiness of that home! Nothing, she realized, in all

66

these years had touched her inmost being, had penetrated to the core of her cold heart like the memories of those early, misty scenes.

One day she wrote a letter to Mrs. Boldin. She, the writer, Madame A. Wynne, had come across a young woman, Amy Kildare, who said that as a girl she had run away from home and now she would like to come back. But she was ashamed to write. Madame Wynne had questioned the girl closely and she was quite sure that this Miss Kildare had in no way incurred shame or disgrace. It had been some time since Madame Wynne had seen the girl but if Mrs. Boldin wished, she would try to find her again—perhaps Mrs. Boldin would like to get in touch with her. The letter ended on a tentative note.

The answer came at once.

My dear Madame Wynne:

My mother told me to write you this letter. She says even if Amy Kildare had done something terrible, she would want her to come home again. My father says so too. My mother says, please find her as soon as you can and tell her to come back. She still misses her. We all miss her. I was a little boy when she left, but though I am in the High School now and play in the school orchestra, I would rather see her than do anything I know. If you see her, be sure to tell her to come right away. My mother says thank you.

Yours respectfully,
Cornelius Boldin

The letter came to the modiste's establishment in

New York. Amy read it and went with it to Madame. "I have had wonderful news," she told her, "I must go away immediately, I can't come back—you may have these last two weeks for nothing." Madame, who had surmised long since the separation, looked curiously at the girl's flushed cheeks, and decided that "Monsieur Ween" had returned. She gave her fatalistic shrug. All Americans were crazy.

"But, yes, Madame,—if you must go—absolument."

When she reached the ferry, Amy looked about her searchingly. "I hope I'm seeing you for the last time— I'm going home, home!" Oh, the unbelievable kindness! She had left them without a word and they still wanted her back!

Eventually she got to Orange and to the little house. She sent a message to Peter's sister and set about her packing. But first she sat down in the little house and looked about her. She would go home, home—how she loved the word, she would stay there a while, but always there was life, still beckoning. It would beckon forever she realized to her adventurousness. Afterwards she would set up an establishment of her own,—she reviewed possibilities—in a rich suburb, where white women would pay and pay for her expertness, caring nothing for realities, only for externals.

"As I myself used to care," she sighed. Her thoughts flashed on. "Then some day I'll work and help with colored people—the only ones who have really cared for and wanted me." Her eyes blurred.

She would never make any attempt to find out who or what she was. If she were white, there would always be people urging her to keep up the silliness of racial prestige. How she hated it all!

"Citizen of the world, that's what I'll be. And now I'll go home."

Peter's sister's little girl came over to be with the pretty lady whom she adored.

"You sit here, Angel, and watch me pack," Amy said, placing her in a little arm-chair. And the baby sat there in silent observation, one tiny leg crossed over the other, surely the quaintest, gravest bit of bronze, Amy thought, that ever lived.

"Miss Amy cried," the child told her mother afterwards.

Perhaps Amy did cry, but if so she was unaware. Certainly she laughed more happily, more spontaneously than she had done for years. Once she got down on her knees in front of the little arm-chair and buried her face in the baby's tiny bosom.

"Oh Angel, Angel," she whispered, "do you suppose Cornelius still plays on that cornet?"

First published in the magazine
The Crisis (Aug–Oct 1920)

CARRIE WILLIAMS CLIFFORD

Friendship

Not by the dusty stretch of days
Slow-gathering to lengthening years
   We measure friendship's chain,
But by the understanding touch,
The smile, the soul-kiss, yea, the tears
   That ease the load of pain.

First published in Carrie Williams Clifford's
collection *The Widening Light* (1922)

OLIVIA WARD BUSH-BANKS

Fancies

Mid parted clouds, all silver-edged,
    A gleam of fiery gold,
A dash of crimson-varied hues,
    The Sunset Story's told.

A mirrored lake 'tween mossy banks,
    A lofty mountain ridge,
A cottage nestling in the vale
    Seen from a ruined bridge.

A woman longing to discern
    Beyond the gleam of gold
A rush of memory, a sigh,
    And Life's strange tale is told.

First published in Olivia Ward
Bush-Bank's collection
Driftwood (1914)

NELLA LARSEN

The Abyss

It began, this next child-bearing, during the morning services of a breathless hot Sunday while the fervent choir soloist was singing: "Ah am freed of mah sorrow," and lasted far into the small hours of Tuesday morning. It seemed, for some reason, not to go off just right. And when, after that long frightfulness, the fourth little dab of amber humanity which Helga had contributed to a despised race was held before her for maternal approval, she failed entirely to respond properly to this sop of consolation, for the suffering and horror through which she had passed. There was from her no pleased, proud smile, no loving, possessive gesture, no manifestation of interest in the important matters of sex and weight. Instead she deliberately closed her eyes, mutely shutting out the sickly infant, its smiling father, the soiled midwife, the curious neighbors, and the tousled room.

A week she lay so. Silent and listless. Ignoring food, the clamoring children, the comings and goings of solicitous, kind-hearted women, her hovering husband, and all of life about her. The neighbors were puzzled. The Reverend Mr. Pleasant Green was worried. The midwife was frightened.

On the floor, in and out among the furniture and under her bed, the twins played. Eager to help, the church-women crowded in and, meeting there others on the same laudable errand, stayed to gossip and to

72

wonder. Anxiously the preacher sat, Bible in hand, beside his wife's bed, or in a nervous half-guilty manner invited the congregated parishioners to join him in prayer for the healing of their sister. Then, kneeling, they would beseech God to stretch out His all-powerful hand on behalf of the afflicted one, softly at first, but with rising vehemence, accompanied by moans and tears, until it seemed that the God to whom they prayed must in mercy to the sufferer grant relief. If only so that she might rise up and escape from the tumult, the heat, and the smell.

Helga, however, was unconcerned, undisturbed by the commotion about her. It was all part of the general unreality. Nothing reached her. Nothing penetrated the kind darkness into which her bruised spirit had retreated. Even that red-letter event, the coming to see her of the old white physician from downtown, who had for a long time stayed talking gravely to her husband, drew from her no interest. Nor for days was she aware that a stranger, a nurse from Mobile, had been added to her household, a brusquely efficient woman who produced order out of chaos and quiet out of bedlam. Neither did the absence of the children, removed by good neighbors at Miss Hartley's insistence, impress her. While she had gone down into that appalling blackness of pain, the ballast of her brain had got loose and she hovered for a long time somewhere in that delightful borderland on the edge of unconsciousness, an enchanted and blissful place where peace and incredible quiet encompassed her.

After weeks she grew better, returned to earth, set her reluctant feet to the hard path of life again.

"Well, here you are!" announced Miss Hartley in her slightly harsh voice one afternoon just before the fall of evening. She had for some time been standing at the bedside gazing down at Helga with an intent speculative look.

"Yes," Helga agreed in a thin little voice, "I'm back." The truth was that she had been back for some hours. Purposely she had lain silent and still, wanting to linger forever in that serene haven, that effortless calm where nothing was expected of her. There she could watch the figures of the past drift by. There was her mother, whom she had loved from a distance and finally so scornfully blamed, who appeared as she had always remembered her, unbelievably beautiful, young, and remote. Robert Anderson, questioning, purposely detached, affecting, as she realized now, her life in a remarkably cruel degree; for at last she understood clearly how deeply, how passionately, she must have loved him. Anne, lovely, secure, wise, selfish. Axel Olsen, conceited, worldly, spoiled. Audrey Denney, placid, taking quietly and without fuss the things which she wanted. James Vayle, snobbish, smug, servile. Mrs. Hayes-Rore, important, kind, determined. The Dahls, rich, correct, climbing. Flashingly, fragmentarily, other long-forgotten figures, women in gay fashionable frocks and men in formal black and white, glided by in bright rooms to distant, vaguely familiar music.

It was refreshingly delicious, this immersion in the past. But it was finished now. It was over. The words of her husband, the Reverend Mr. Pleasant Green, who had been standing at the window looking mournfully out at the scorched melon-patch, ruined because Helga had been ill so long and unable to tend it, were confirmation of that.

"The Lord be praised," he said, and came forward. It was distinctly disagreeable. It was even more

74

disagreeable to feel his moist hand on hers. A cold shiver brushed over her. She closed her eyes. Obstinately and with all her small strength she drew her hand away from him. Hid it far down under the bedcovering, and turned her face away to hide a grimace of unconquerable aversion. She cared nothing, at that moment, for his hurt surprise. She knew only that, in the hideous agony that for interminable hours—no, centuries—she had borne, the luster of religion had vanished; that revulsion had come upon her; that she hated this man. Between them the vastness of the universe had come.

Miss Hartley, all-seeing and instantly aware of a situation, as she had been quite aware that her patient had been conscious for some time before she herself had announced the fact, intervened, saying firmly: "I think it might be better if you didn't try to talk to her now. She's terribly sick and weak yet. She's still got some fever and we mustn't excite her or she's liable to slip back. And we don't want that, do we?"

No, the man, her husband, responded, they didn't want that. Reluctantly he went from the room with a last look at Helga, who was lying on her back with one frail, pale hand under her small head, her curly black hair scattered loose on the pillow. She regarded him from behind dropped lids. The day was hot, her breasts were covered only by a nightgown of filmy *crêpe*, a relic of prematrimonial days, which had slipped from one carved shoulder. He flinched. Helga's petulant lip curled, for she well knew that this fresh reminder of her desirability was like the flick of a whip.

Miss Hartley carefully closed the door after the retreating husband. "It's time," she said, "for your evening treatment, and then you've got to try to sleep for a while. No more visitors tonight."

Helga nodded and tried unsuccessfully to make a little smile. She was glad of Miss Hartley's presence. It would, she felt, protect her from so much. She mustn't, she thought to herself, get well too fast. Since it seemed she was going to get well. In bed she could think, could have a certain amount of quiet. Of aloneness.

In that period of racking pain and calamitous fright Helga had learned what passion and credulity could do to one. In her was born angry bitterness and an enormous disgust. The cruel, unrelieved suffering had beaten down her protective wall of artificial faith in the infinite wisdom, in the mercy, of God. For had she not called in her agony on Him? And He had not heard. Why? Because, she knew now, He wasn't there. Didn't exist. Into that yawning gap of unspeakable brutality had gone, too, her belief in the miracle and wonder of life. Only scorn, resentment, and hate remained—and ridicule. Life wasn't a miracle, a wonder. It was, for Negroes at least, only a great disappointment. Something to be got through with as best one could. No one was interested in them or helped them. God! Bah! And they were only a nuisance to other people.

Everything in her mind was hot and cold, beating and swirling about. Within her emaciated body raged disillusion. Chaotic turmoil. With the obscuring curtain of religion rent, she was able to look about her and see with shocked eyes this thing that she had done to herself. She couldn't, she thought ironically, even blame God for it, now that she knew that He didn't exist. No. No more than she could pray to Him for the death of her husband, the Reverend Mr. Pleasant Green. The white man's God. And His great love for all people regardless of race! What idiotic nonsense she had allowed herself to believe. How could she, how could anyone, have been so deluded? How could ten million black folk credit it when daily before their eyes was enacted its contradiction? Not that she at all cared about the ten million. But herself. Her sons. Her daughter. These would grow to manhood, to woman-hood, in this vicious, this hypocritical land. The dark eyes filled with tears.

"I wouldn't," the nurse advised, "do that. You've been dreadfully sick, you know. I can't have you worry-ing. Time enough for that when you're well. Now you must sleep all you possibly can."

Helga did sleep. She found it surprisingly easy to sleep. Aided by Miss Hartley's rather masterful discern-ment, she took advantage of the ease with which this blessed enchantment stole over her. From her hus-band's praisings, prayers, and caresses she sought refuge in sleep, and from the neighbors' gifts, advice, and sympathy.

There was the day on which they told her that the last sickly infant, born of such futile torture and linger-ing torment, had died after a short week of slight living. Just closed his eyes and died. No vitality. On hearing it Helga too had just closed her eyes. Not to die. She was convinced that before her there were years of living. Perhaps of happiness even. For a new idea had come to her. She had closed her eyes to shut in any telltale gleam of the relief which she felt. One less. And she had gone off into sleep.

And there was that Sunday morning on which the Reverend Mr. Pleasant Green had informed her that they were that day to hold a special thanksgiving service for her recovery. There would, he said, be prayers, special testimonies, and songs. Was there anything particular she would like to have said, to have prayed for, to have sung? Helga had smiled from sheer amusement as she replied that there was nothing. Nothing at all. She only hoped that they would enjoy themselves. And, closing her eyes that he might be discouraged from longer tarrying, she had gone off to sleep.

Waking later to the sound of joyous religious abandon floating in through the opened windows, she had asked a little diffidently that she be allowed to read. Miss Hartley's sketchy brows contracted into a dubious frown. After a judicious pause she had answered: "No, I don't think so." Then, seeing the rebellious tears which had sprung into her patient's eyes, she added kindly: "But I'll read to you a little if you like."

That, Helga replied, would be nice. In the next room on a high-up shelf was a book. She'd forgotten the name, but its author was Anatole France. There was a story, "The Procurator of Judea." Would Miss Hartley read that? "Thanks. Thanks awfully."

"'Lælius Lamia, born in Italy of illustrious parents,'" began the nurse in her slightly harsh voice.

Helga drank it in.

"'. . . For to this day the women bring down doves to the altar as their victims . . .'"

Helga closed her eyes.

"'. . . Africa and Asia have already enriched us with a considerable number of gods . . .'"

Miss Hartley looked up. Helga had slipped into slumber while the superbly ironic ending which she had so desired to hear was yet a long way off. A dull tale, was Miss Hartley's opinion, as she curiously turned the pages to see how it turned out.

"'Jesus? . . . Jesus—of Nazareth? I cannot call him to mind.'"

"Huh!" she muttered, puzzled. "Silly." And closed the book.

CLARA ANN THOMPSON

Hope

The saddest day will have an eve,
    The darkest night, a morn;
Think not, when clouds are thick and dark,
    Thy way is too forlorn.

For, ev'ry cloud that e'er did rise,
    To shade thy life's bright way,
And ev'ry restless night of pain,
    And ev'ry weary day,

Will bring thee gifts, thou'lt value more,
    Because they cost so dear;
The soul that faints not in the storm,
    Emerges bright and clear.

First published in Clara Ann
Thompson's collection *Songs
from the Wayside* (1908)

The Lights at Carney's Point*

O white little lights at Carney's Point,
     You shine so clear o'er the Delaware;
When the moon rides high in the silver sky,
     Then you gleam, white gems on the Delaware.
Diamond circlet on a full white throat,
     You laugh your rays on a questing boat;
Is it peace you dream in your flashing gleam,
      O'er the quiet flow of the Delaware?

And the lights grew dim at the water's brim,
      For the smoke of the mills shredded slow
        between;
And the smoke was red, as is new bloodshed,
      And the lights went lurid 'neath the livid
        screen.

O red little lights at Carney's Point,
     You glower so grim o'er the Delaware;
When the moon hides low sombrous clouds below,
     Then you glow like coals o'er the Delaware.
Blood red rubies on a throat of fire,
     You flash through the dusk of a funeral pyre;
Are there hearth fires red whom you fear and dread
     O'er the turgid flow of the Delaware?

* The lights of the great powder mills at Carney's Point can be seen
for miles across and down the river.

And the lights gleamed gold o'er the river cold,
    For the murk of the furnace shed a copper veil;
And the veil was grim at the great cloud's brim,
    And the lights went molten, now hot, now pale.

O gold little lights at Carney's Point,
    You gleam so proud o'er the Delaware;
When the moon grows wan in the eastering dawn,
    Then you sparkle gold points o'er the
        Delaware.
Aureate filagree on a Croesus' brow,
    You hasten the dawn on a gray ship's prow.
Light you streams of gold in the grim ship's hold
    O'er the sullen flow of the Delaware?

And the lights went gray in the ash of day,
    For a quiet Aurora brought a halcyon balm;
And the sun laughed high in the infinite sky,
    And the lights were forgot in the sweet, sane
        calm.

First published in *The Dunbar Speaker
and Entertainer*, an anthology edited by
Alice Dunbar-Nelson (1920)

Angelina Weld Grimké

The Closing Door

I was fifteen at the time, diffident and old far beyond my years from much knocking about from pillar to post, a yellow, scrawny, unbeautiful girl, when the big heart of Agnes Milton took pity upon me, loved me and brought me home to live with her in her tiny, sun-filled flat. We were only distantly related, very distantly, in fact, on my dead father's side. You can see, then, there was no binding bloodtie between us, that she was under absolutely no obligation to do what she did. I have wondered time and again how many women would have opened their hearts and their homes, as Agnes Milton did, to a forlorn, unattractive, homeless girl-woman. That one fine, free, generous act of hers alone shows the wonder-quality of her soul.

Just one little word to explain me. After my father had taken one last cup too many and they had carried him, for the last time, out of the house into which he had been carried so often, my mother, being compelled to work again, returned to the rich family with whom she had been a maid before her marriage. She regarded me as seriously, I suppose, as she did anything in this world; but as it was impossible to have me with her I was passed along from one of her relatives to another. When one tired of me, on I went to the next. Well, I can say this for each and all of them, they certainly believed in teaching me how to work! Judging by the number of homes in which I lived until I was fifteen, my mother was rich indeed in one possession—an abundance of relatives.

And then came Agnes Milton.

Have you ever, I wonder, known a happy person? I mean a really happy one? He is as rare as a white blackbird in this sombre-faced world of ours. I have know two and only two. They were Agnes Milton and her husband Jim. And their happiness did not last. Jim was a brown, good-natured giant with a slow, most attractive smile and gleaming teeth. He spoke always in a deep sad drawl, and you would have thought him the most unhappy person imaginable until you glimpsed his black eyes fairly twinkling under their half-closed lids. He made money—what is called "easy money"—by playing rag-time for dances. He was one of a troupe that are called "social entertainers." As far as Jim was concerned, it would have slipped away in just as easy a manner, if it hadn't been for Agnes. For she, in spite of all her seeming carefree joyousness was a thrifty soul. As long as Jim could have good food and plenty of it, now and then the theatre, a concert or a dance, and his gold-tipped ciga-rettes, he didn't care what became of his money.

"Oh, Ag!"

If I close my eyes I can hear his slow sad voice as clearly as though these ten long years had not passed by. I can hear the click of the patent lock as he closed the flat door. I can hear the bang of his hat as he hung it on the rack. I can get the whiff of his cigarette.

"Oh, Ag!"

"That you, Jim?" I can see Agnes' happy eyes and hear her eager, soft voice.

And then after a pause, that sad voice:

"No, Ag!"

84

I can hear her delighted little chuckle. She very seldom laughed outright.

"Where are you, anyway?" It was the plaintive voice again.

"Here!"

And then he'd make believe he couldn't find her and go hunting her all over that tiny flat, searching for her in every room he knew she was not. And he'd stumble over things in pretended excitement and haste and grunt and swear all in that inimitable slow way of his. And she'd stand there, her eyes shining and every once in a while giving that dear little chuckle of hers.

Finally he'd appear in the door panting and disheveled and would look at her in pretended intense surprise for a second, and then he'd say in an aggrieved voice:

"'S not fair, Agnes! 'S not fair!"

She wouldn't say a word, just stand there smiling at him. After a little, slowly, he'd begin to smile too.

That smile of theirs was one of the most beautiful things I have ever seen and each meeting it was the same. Their joy and love seemed to gush up and bubble over through their lips and eyes.

Presently he'd say:

"Catch!"

She'd hold up her little white apron by the corners and he'd put his hand in his pocket and bring out sometimes a big, sometimes a little, wad of greenbacks and toss it to her and she'd catch it, too, I can tell you. And her eyes would beam and dance at him over it. Oh! she didn't love the money for itself but him for trusting her with it.

For fear you may not understand I must tell you no more generous soul ever lived than Agnes Milton. Look

85

at what she did for me. And she was always giving a nickel or a dime to some child, flowers or fruit to a sick woman, money to tide over a friend. No beggar was ever turned away empty, from her flat. But she managed, somehow, to increase her little hoard in the bank against that possible rainy day.

Well, to return. At this juncture, Jim would say oh! so sadly his eyes fairly twinkling:

"Please, m'a'm, do I get paid today too?"

And then she'd screw up her mouth and twist her head to the side and look at him and say in a most judicial manner:

"Well, now, I really can't say as to that. It strikes me you'll have to find that out for yourself."

Oh! they didn't mind me. He would reach her, it seemed, in one stride and would pick her up bodily, apron, money and all. After a space, she'd disentangle herself and say sternly, shaking the while her little forefinger before his delighted eyes:

"Jim Milton, you've overdrawn your wages again."

And then he'd look oh! so contrite and so upset and so shocked at being caught in such a gigantic piece of attempted fraud.

"No?" he'd say. If you only could have heard the mournful drawl of him.

"No? Now, is that so? I'm really at heart an honest, hard-working man. I'll have to pay it back."

He did. I can vouch for it.

Sometimes after this, he'd swing her up onto his shoulder and they'd go dashing and prancing and shrieking and laughing all over the little flat. Once after I had seen scared faces appearing at various windows, at times like these, I used to rush around and shut the windows down tight. Two happy children, that's what they were then—younger even than I.

There was just the merest suspicion of a cloud over their happiness, these days; they had been married five years and had no children.

It was the mother heart of Agnes that had yearned over me, had pity upon me, loved me and brought me to live in the only home I have ever known. I have cared for people. I care for Jim; but Agnes Milton is the only person I have ever really loved. I love her still. And before it was too late, I used to pray that in some way I might change places with her and go into that darkness where though, still living, one forgets sun and moon and stars and flowers and winds—and love itself, and existence means dark, foul-smelling cages, hollow clanging doors, hollow monotonous days. But a month ago when Jim and I went to see her, she had changed—she had receded even from us. She seemed—how can I express it?—blank, empty, a grey automaton, a mere shell. No soul looked out at us through her vacant eyes.

We did not utter a word during our long journey homeward. Jim had unlocked the door before I spoke.

"Jim," I said, "they may still have the poor husk of her cooped up there but her soul, thank God, at least for that, is free at last!"

And Jim, I cannot tell of his face, said never a word but turned away and went heavily down the stairs. And I, I went into Agnes Milton's flat and closed the door. You would never have dreamed it was the same place. For a long time I stood amid all the brightness and mockery of her sun-drenched rooms. And I prayed. Night and day I have prayed since, the same prayer—that God, if he knows any pity at all may soon, soon release the poor spent body of hers.

I wish I might show you Agnes Milton of those far off happy days. She wasn't tall and she wasn't short; she wasn't stout and she wasn't thin. Her back was straight and her head high. She was rather graceful, I thought. In coloring she was Spanish or Italian. Her hair was not very long but it was soft and silky and black. Her features were not too sharp, her eyes clear and dark, a warm leaf brown in fact. Her mouth was really beautiful. This doesn't give her I find. It was the shining beauty and gayety of her soul that lighted up her whole body and somehow made her her. And she was generally smiling or chuckling. Her eyes almost closed when she did so and there were the most delightful crinkles all about them. Under her left eye there was a small scar, a reminder of some childhood escapade, that became, when she smiled, the most adorable of dimples.

One day, I remember, we were standing at the window in the bright sunlight. Some excitement in the street below had drawn us. I turned to her—the reason has gone from me now—and called out suddenly:

"Agnes Milton!"

"Heavens! What is it?"

"Why, you're wrinkling!"

"Wrinkling! Where?" And she began inspecting the smooth freshness of her housedress.

"No, your face," I exclaimed. "Honest! Stand still there in that light. Now! Just look at them all around your eyes."

She chuckled.

"How you ever expect me to see them I don't know, without a glass or anything!"

And her face crinkled up into a smile.

"There! That's it!—That's how you get them."

"How?"

"Smiling too much."

"Oh, no! Lucy, child, that's impossible."

"How do you mean impossible? You didn't get them that way? Just wait till I get a glass."

"No, don't," and she stopped me with a detaining hand. "I'm not doubting you. What I mean is—it's absolutely impossible to smile too much."

I felt my eyes stretching with surprise.

"You mean," I said, "you don't mind being wrinkled? You, a woman?"

She shook her head at me many times, smiling and chuckling softly the while.

"Not the very littlest, tiniest bit—not this much," and she showed me just the barest tip of her pink tongue between her white teeth. She smiled, then, and there was the dimple.

"And you only twenty-five?" I exclaimed.

She didn't answer for a moment and when she did she spoke quietly:

"Lucy, child, we've all got to wrinkle sometime, somehow, if we live long enough. I'd much rather know mine were smile ones than frown ones." She waited a second and then looked at me with her beautiful clear eyes and added, "Wouldn't you?"

For reply I leaned forward and kissed them. I loved them from that time on.

Here is another memory of her—perhaps the loveliest of them all and yet, as you will see, tingled with the first sadness. It came near the end of our happy days. It was a May dusk. I had been sewing all the afternoon and was as close to the window as I could get to catch the last of the failing light. I was trying to thread a needle— had been trying for several minutes, in fact, and was just in the very act of succeeding when two soft hands were clapped over my eyes.

"Oh, Agnes!" I said none too pleasantly. It was provoking. "There! You've made me lose my needle."

"Bother your old needle, cross patch!" she said close to my ear. She still held her hands over my eyes.

I waited a moment or so.

"Well," I said, "what's the idea?"

"Please don't be cross," came the soft voice still close to my ear.

"I'm not."

At that she chuckled.

"Well!" I said.

"I'm trying to tell you something. Sh! not so loud."

"Well, go ahead then; and why must I sh!"

"Because you must."

I waited.

"Well!' I said a third time, but in a whisper to humor her. We were alone in the flat, there was no reason I could see for this tremendous secrecy.

"I'm waiting for you to be sweet to me."

"I am. But why I should have to lose my needle and my temper and be blinded and sweet just to hear something—is beyond me."

"Because I don't wish you to see me while I say it." Her soft lips were kissing my ear.

"Well, I'm very sweet now. What is it?"

There was another little pause and during it her fingers over my eyes trembled a little. She was breathing quicker too.

"Agnes Milton, what *is* it?"

"Wait, I'm just trying to think *how* to tell you. Are you sure you're very sweet?"

"Sure."

I loved the feel of her hands and sat very still.

"Lucy!"

"Yes."

"What do you think would be the loveliest, loveliest thing for you to know was—was—there—close—just under your heart?"

But I waited for no more. I took her hands from my eyes and turned to look at her. The beauty of her face made me catch my breath.

At last I said:

"You mean—" I didn't need to finish.

"Yes! Yes! And I'm so happy, happy, happy! And so is Jim."

"Agnes, oh my dear, and so am I!" And I kissed her two dear eyes. "But why mustn't I whoop? I've simply got to," I added.

"No! No! No! Oh, sh!" And for the very first time I saw fear in her eyes.

"Agnes," I said, "what is it?"

"I'm—I'm just a little afraid, I believe."

"Afraid!" I had cried out in surprise.

"Sh! Lucy!—Yes."

"But of what?" I spoke in a half whisper too. "You mean you're afraid you may die?"

"Oh, no, not that."

"What, then?"

"Lucy," her answer came slowly, a little abstractedly, "there's—such—a thing—as being—*too* happy,—*too* happy."

"Nonsense," I answered.

But she only shook her head at me slowly many times and her great wistful eyes came to mine and seemed to cling to them. It made my heart fairly ache and I turned my head away so that she couldn't see her fears were affecting me. And then quite suddenly I felt a disagreeable little chill run up and down my back.

"Lucy," she said after a little.

"Yes," I was looking out of the window and not at her.

Do you remember Kipling's "Without Benefit of Clergy?"

I did and I said so. Agnes had Kipling bound in ten beautiful volumes. She loved him. At first that had been enough for me, and then I had come to love him for himself. I had read all of those ten volumes through from cover to cover, poety and all.

"You haven't forgotten Ameera, then?"

"No."

"Poor Ameera!" She was thoughtful a moment and then went on: "She knew what it was to be too happy. Do you remember what she said once to Holden?"

Again I felt that queer little shiver.

"She said many things, as I remember, Agnes. Which?"

"This was after Tota's death."

"Well!"

"They were on the roof—she and Holden—under the night." Her eyes suddenly widened and darkened and then she went on:

She turned to Holden and said: "'We must make no protestations of delight but go softly underneath the stars, lest God find us out.'" She paused. "Do you remember?"

"Yes," I answered; but I couldn't look at her.

"Well," she spoke slowly and quietly, "I have a feeling here, Lucy," and she placed her left hand against her heart, "here, that Jim and you and I must go softly—very softly—underneath the stars."

Again I felt that unpleasant chill up and down my back.

She stood just where she was for a little space, her hand still against her heart and her eyes wide, dark and unseeing, fixed straight ahead of her. Then suddenly and without a sound she turned and went towards the door and opened it.

I started to follow her; but she put up her hand.

"No, Lucy, please—I wish to be alone—for a little."

And with that she went and shut the door very slowly, quite noiselessly behind her. The closing was so slow, so silent, that I could not tell just when it shut. I found myself trembling violently. A sudden and inexplicable terror filled me as that door closed behind her.

We were to become accustomed to it, Jim and I, as much as it was possible to do so, in those terrible days that were to follow. We were to become used to entering a room in search of Agnes, only to find it empty and the door opposite closing, closing, almost imperceptibly, noiselessly—and, yes, at last irrevocably—between us. And each time it happened the terror was as fresh upon me as at the very first.

The days that immediately followed I cannot say were really unhappy ones. More to humor Agnes at first than anything else "we went softly." But as time passed even we became infected. Literally and figuratively we began to go "softly under the stars." We came to feel that each of us moved ever with a finger to his lips. There came

93

to be also a sort of expectancy upon us, a listening, a waiting. Even the neighbors noticed the difference. Jim still played his ragtime and sang, but softly; we laughed and joked, but quietly. We got so we even washed the dishes and pots and pans quietly. Sometimes Jim and I forgot, but as certainly as we did there was Agnes in the door, dark-eyed, a little pale and her, "Oh, Jim!—Oh, Lucy! Sh!"

I haven't spoken of this before because it wasn't necessary. Agnes had a brother called Bob. He was her favorite of all her brothers and sisters. He was younger than she, five years, I think, a handsome, harum-scarum, happy-go-lucky, restless, reckless daredevil, but sweet-tempered and good hearted and lovable withal. I don't believe he knew what fear was. His home was in Mississippi, a small town there. It was the family home, in fact. Agnes had lived there herself until she was seventeen or eighteen. He had visited us two or three times and you can imagine the pande-monium that reigned at such times, for he had come during our happy days. Well, he was very fond of Agnes and, as irresponsible as he seemed, one thing he never failed to do and that was to write her a letter every single week. Each Tuesday morning, just like clockwork, the very first mail there was his letter. Other mornings Agnes was not so particular; but Tuesday mornings she always went herself to the mail-box in the hall.

It was a Tuesday morning about four months, maybe, after my first experience with the closing door. The bell rang three times, the postman's signal when he had left a letter, Agnes came to her feet, her eyes sparkling:

"My letter from Bob," she said and made for the door.

She came back slowly, I noticed, and her face was a little pale and worried. She had an opened and an unopened letter in her hand.

"Well, what does Bob say?" I asked.

"This—this isn't from Bob," she said slowly. "It's only a bill."

"Well, go ahead and open his letter," I said.

"There—there wasn't any, Lucy."

"What!" I exclaimed. I was surprised.

"No. I don't know what it means."

"It will come probably in the second mail," I said. "It has sometimes."

"Yes," she said, I thought rather listlessly.

It didn't come in the second mail nor in the third.

"Agnes," I said. "There's some good explanation. It's not like Bob to fail you."

"No."

"He's busy or got a girl maybe."

She was a little jealous of him and I hoped this last would rouse her, but it didn't.

"Yes, maybe that's it," she said without any life.

"Well, I hope you're not going to let this interfere with your walk," I said.

"I had thought—" she began, but I cut her off.

"You promised Jim you'd go out every single day," I reminded her.

"All right, Agnes Milton's conscience," she said smiling a little. "I'll go, then."

She hadn't been gone fifteen minutes when the electric bell began shrilling continuously throughout the flat.

Somehow I knew it meant trouble. My mind

immediately flew to Agnes. It took me a second or so to get myself together and then I went to the tube.

"Well," I called. My voice sounded strange and high.

A boy's voice answered:

"Lady here named Mrs. James Milton?"

"Yes." I managed to say.

"Telegram fo' you'se."

It wasn't Agnes, after all. I drew a deep breath. Nothing else seemed to matter for a minute.

"Say!" the voice called up from below. "Wot's de mattah wid you'se up dere?"

"Bring it up," I said at last. "Third floor, front."

I opened the door and waited.

The boy was taking his time and whistling as he came.

"Here!" I called out as he reached our floor.

It was inside his cap and he had to take it off to give it to me.

I saw him eyeing me rather curiously.

"You Mrs. Milton?" he asked.

"No, but this is her flat. I'll sign for it. She's out. Where do I sign? There? Have you a pencil?"

With the door shut behind me again, I began to think out what I had better do. Jim was not to be home until late that night. Within five minutes I had decided. I tore open the yellow envelope and read the message.

It ran: "Bob died suddenly. Under no circumstances come. Father."

The rest of that day was a nightmare to me. I concealed the telegram in my waist. Agnes came home finally and was so alarmed at my appearance, I pleaded a frightful sick headache and went to bed. When Jim came home late that night Agnes was asleep. I caught him in the

96

hall and gave him the telegram. She had to be told, we decided, because a letter from Mississippi might come at any time. He broke it to her the next morning. We were all hard hit, but Agnes from that time on was a changed woman.

Day after day dragged by and the letter of explanation did not come. It was strange, to say the least.

The Sunday afternoon following, we were all sitting, after dinner, in the little parlor. None of us had been saying much.

Suddenly Agnes said:

"Jim!"

"Yes!"

"Wasn't it strange that father never said how or when Bob died?"

"Would have made the telegram too long and expensive, perhaps," Jim replied.

We were all thinking, in the pause that followed, the same thing, I dare say. Agnes' father was not poor and it did seem he might have done that much.

"And why, do you suppose I was not to come under any circumstances? And why don't they write?"

Just then the bell rang and there was no chance for a reply.

Jim got up in his leisurely way and went to the tube.

Agnes and I both listened—a little tensely, I remember.

"Yes!" we heard Jim say, and then with spaces in between:

"Joe?—Joe who?—I think you must have made a mistake. No, I can't say that I do know anyone called Joe. What? Milton? Yes, that's my name! What? Oh! Brooks. Joe Brooks?—"

But Agnes waited for no more. She rushed by me into the hall.

"Jim! Jim! It's my brother Joe."

"Look here! Are you Agnes' brother, Joe?" Jim called quickly for him. "Great Jehoshaphat! Man! Come up! What a mess I've made of this."

For the first time I saw Jim move quickly. Within a second he was out of the flat and running down the stairs. Agnes followed to the stairhead and waited there. I went back into the little parlor for I had followed her into the hall, and sat down and waited.

They all came in presently. Joe was older than Agnes but looked very much like her. He was thin, his face really haggard and his hair quite grey. I found out afterward that he was in his early thirties but he appeared much older. He was smiling, but the smile did not reach his eyes. They were strange aloof eyes. They rested on you and yet seemed to see something beyond. You felt as though they had looked upon something that could never be forgotten. When he was not smiling his face was grim, the chin firm and set. He was a man of very few words, I found.

Agnes and Jim were both talking at once and he answered them now and then in monosyllables. Agnes introduced us. He shook hands, I thought in rather a perfunctory way, without saying anything, and we all sat down.

We steered clear quite deliberately from the thoughts uppermost in all our minds. We spoke of his journey, when he left Mississippi, the length of time it had taken him to come and the weather. Suddenly Agnes jumped up:

"Joe, aren't you famished?"

"Well, I wouldn't mind a little something, Agnes," he answered, and then he added:

"I'm not as starved as I was traveling in the South; but I have kind of a hollow feeling."

"What do you mean?" she asked.

"Jim-Crow cars," he answered laconically.

"I'd forgotten," she said. "I've been away so long."

He made no reply.

"Aren't conditions any better at all?" she asked after a little.

"No, I can't say as they are."

None of us said anything. She stood there a minute or so, pulling away at the frill on her apron. She stopped suddenly, drew a long breath, and said:

"I wish you all could move away, Jim, and come North."

For one second before he lowered his eyes I saw a strange gleam in them. He seemed to be examining his shoes carefully from all angles. His jaw looked grimmer than ever and I saw a flickering of the muscles in his cheeks.

"That would be nice," he said at last and then added, "but we can't, Agnes. I like my coffee strong, please."

"Joe," she said, going to the door. "I'm sorry, I was forgetting."

I rose at that.

"Agnes, let me go. You stay here."

She hesitated, but Joe spoke up:

"No, Agnes, you go. I know your cooking."

You could have heard a pin drop for a minute. Jim looked queer and so did Agnes for a second and then she tried to laugh it off.

99

"Don't mind Joe. He doesn't mean anything. He always was like that."

And then she left us.

Well, I was hurt. Joe made no attempt to apologize or anything. He even seemed to have forgotten me. Jim looked at me and smiled, his nice smile, but I was really hurt. I came to understand, however, later. Presently Joe said:

"About Agnes! We hadn't been told anything!"

"Didn't she write about it?"

"No."

"Wanted to surprise you, I guess."

"How long?" Joe asked after a little.

"Before?"

"Yes."

"Four months, I should say."

"That complicates matters some."

I got up to leave. I was so evidently in the way.

Joe looked up quietly and said:

"Oh! don't go! It isn't necessary."

I sat down again.

"No, Lucy, stay." Jim added, "What do you mean 'complicates'?"

Joe examined his shoes for several moments and then looked up suddenly.

"Just where is Agnes?"

"In the kitchen, I guess." Jim looked a trifle surprised.

"Where is that?"

"The other end of the flat near the door."

"She can't possibly hear anything, then?"

"No."

"Well, then, listen Jim, and you, what's your name?

100

Lucy? Well, Lucy, then. Listen carefully, you two, to every single word I am going to say." He frowned a few moments at his shoes and then went on: "Bob went out fishing in the woods near his shack; spent the night there; slept in wet clothes; it had been raining all day; came home; contracted double pneumonia and died in two days' time. Have you that?"

We both nodded. "That's the story we are to tell Agnes."

Jim had his mouth open to ask something, when Agnes came in. She had very evidently not heard anything, however, for there was a little color in her face and it was just a little happy again.

"I've been thinking about you, Joe," she said. "What on earth are you getting so grey for?"

"Grey!" he exclaimed. "Am I grey?" There was no doubt about it, his surprise was genuine.

"Didn't you know it?" She chuckled a little. It was the first time in days.

"No, I didn't."

She made him get up, at that, and drew him to the oval glass over the mantel.

"Don't you ever look at yourself, Joe?"

"Not much, that's the truth." I could see his face in the mirror from where I sat. His eyes widened a trifle. I saw, and then he turned away abruptly and sat down again. He made no comment. Agnes broke the rather little silence that followed.

"Joe!"

"Yes!"

"You haven't been sick or anything, have you?"

"No, why?"

"You seem so much thinner. When I last saw you you were almost stout."

"That's some years ago, Agnes."

"Yes, but one ought to get stouter not thinner with age."

Again I caught that strange gleam in his eyes before he lowered them. For a moment he sat perfectly still without answering.

"You can put it down to hard work, if you like, Agnes. Isn't that my coffee I smell boiling over?"

"Yes, I believe it is. I just ran in to tell you I'll be ready for you in about ten minutes."

She went out hastily but took time to pull the portière across the door. I thought it strange at the time and looked at Jim. He didn't seem to notice it, however, but waited, I saw, until he had heard Agnes' heel taps going into the kitchen.

"Now," he said, "what do you mean when you say that is the story we are to tell Agnes?"

"Just that."

"You mean—" he paused "that it isn't true?"

"No, it isn't true."

"Bob didn't die that way?"

"No."

I felt myself stiffening in my chair and my two hands gripping the two arms of my chair tightly. I looked at Jim. I sensed the same tensioning in him. There was a long pause. Joe was examining his shoes again. The flickering in his cheeks I saw was more noticeable.

Finally Jim brought out just one word:

"How?"

"There was a little trouble," he began and then paused so long Jim said:

"You mean he was—injured in some way?"

Joe looked up suddenly at Jim, at that, and then down again. But his expression even in that fleeting glance set me to trembling all over. Jim, I saw, had been affected too. He sat stiffly bent forward. He had been in the act of raising his cigarette to his lips and his arm seemed as though frozen in mid-air.

"Yes," he said, "injured." But the way in which he said "injured" made me tremble all the more.

Again there was a pause and again Jim broke it with his one word:

"How?"

"You don't read the papers, I see," Joe said.

"Yes, I read them."

"It was in all the papers."

"I missed it, then."

"Yes."

It was quiet again for a little.

"Have you ever lived in the South?" Joe asked.

"No."

"Nice civilized place, the South," Joe said.

And again I found myself trembling violently. I had to fight with might and main to keep my teeth from chattering. And yet it was not what he had said but his tone again.

"I hadn't so heard it described," Jim said after a little.

"No?—you didn't know, I suppose, that there is an unwritten law in the South that when a colored and a white person meet on the sidewalk, the colored person must get off into the street until the white one passes?"

"No, I hadn't heard of it."

"Well, it's so. That was the little trouble."

"You mean—"

"Bob refused to get off the sidewalk."

"Well?"

"The white man pushed him off. Bob knocked him down. The white man attempted to teach the 'damned nigger' a lesson." Again he paused.

"Well?"

"The lesson didn't end properly. Bob all but killed him."

It was so still in that room that although Jim was sitting across the room I could hear his watch ticking distinctly in his vest pocket. I had been holding my breath and when I was forced to expel it, the sound was so loud they both turned quickly towards me, startled for the second.

"That would have been Bob." It was Jim speaking.

"Yes."

"I suppose it didn't end there?"

"No."

"Go on, Joe." Even Jim's voice sounded strained and strange.

And Joe went on. He never raised his voice, never lowered it. Throughout, his tone was entirely colorless. And yet as though it had been seared into my very soul I remember word for word, everything he said.

"An orderly mob, in an orderly manner, on a Sunday morning—I am quoting the newspapers—broke into the jail, took him out, slung him up to the limb of a tree, riddled his body with bullets, saturated it with coal oil, lighted a fire underneath him, gouged out his eyes with red hot irons, burnt him to a crisp and then sold souvenirs of him, ears, fingers, toes. His teeth brought five dollars each." He ceased for a moment.

"He is still hanging on that tree.—We are not allowed to have even what is left."

There was a roaring in my ears. I seemed to be a long way off. I was sinking into a horrible black vortex that seemed to be sucking me down. I opened my eyes and saw Jim dimly. His nostrils seemed to be two black wide holes. His face was taut, every line set. I saw him draw a great deep breath. The blackness sucked me down still deeper. And then suddenly I found myself on my feet struggling against that hideous darkness and I heard my own voice as from a great distance calling out over and over again, "Oh, my God! Oh, my God! Oh, my God!"

They both came running to me, but I should have fainted for the first and only time in my life but that I heard suddenly above those strange noises in my ears a little choking, strangling sound. It revived me instantly. I broke from them and tried to get to the door.

"Agnes! Agnes!" I called out.

But they were before me. Jim tore the portière aside. They caught her just as she was falling.

She lay unconscious for hours. When he did come to, she found all three of us about her bed. Her bewildered eyes went from Jim's face to mine and then to Joe's. They paused there; she frowned a little. And then we saw the whole thing slowly come back to her. She groaned and closed her eyes. Joe started to leave the room but she opened her eyes quickly and indicated that he was not to go. He came back. Again she closed her eyes.

And then she began to grow restless.

"Agnes!" I asked, "Is there anything you want?"

She quieted a little under my voice.

"No," she said. "No."

Presently she opened her eyes again. They were very bright. She looked at each of us in turn a second time.

Then she said:

"I've had to live all this time to find out."

"Find out what, Agnes?" It was Jim's voice.

"Why I'm here—why I'm here."

"Yes, of course." Jim spoke oh! so gently, humoring her. His hand was smoothing away the damp little curls about her forehead.

"It's no use your making believe you understand, you don't." It was the first time I had ever heard her speak irritably to Jim. She moved her head away from his hand.

His eyes were a little hurt and he took his hand away.

"No." His voice was as gentle as ever. "I don't understand, then."

There was a pause and then she said abruptly:

"I'm an instrument."

No one answered her.

"That's all—an instrument."

We merely watched her.

"One of the many."

And then Jim in his kindly blundering way made his second mistake.

"Yes, Agnes," he said. "Yes."

But at that, she took even me by surprise. She sat up in bed suddenly, her eyes wild and staring and before we could stop her, began beating her breast.

"Agnes," I said. "Don't! Don't!"

"I shall," she said in a strange high voice.

Well, we let her alone. It would have meant a struggle.

And then amid little sobbing breaths, beating her breast the while, she began to cry out: "Yes!—Yes!—I!—I!—An instrument of reproduction!—another of the many!—a colored woman—doomed!—cursed!—put here!—willing or unwilling! For what?—to bring children here—men children—for the sport—the lust—of possible orderly mobs—who go about things—in an orderly manner—on Sunday mornings!"

"Agnes," I cried out. "Agnes! Your child will be born in the North. He need never go South."

She had listened to me at any rate.

"Yes," she said, "in the North. In the North.—And have there been no lynchings in the North?"

I was silenced.

"The North permits it too," she cried. "The North is silent as well as the South."

And then as she sat there her eyes became less wild but more terrible. They became the eyes of a seeress. When she spoke again she spoke loudly, clearly, slowly:

"There is a time coming—and soon—when no colored man—no colored woman—no colored child, born or unborn—will be safe—in this country."

"Oh Agnes," I cried again. "Sh! sh!"

She turned her terrible eyes upon me.

"There is no more need for silence—in this house. God has found us out."

"Oh Agnes," the tears were frankly running down my cheeks. "We must believe that God is very pitiful. We must. He will find a way."

She waited a moment and said simply:

"Will He?"

"Yes, Agnes! Yes!"

"I will believe you, then. I will give Him one more chance. Then, if He is not pitiful, then if He is not pitiful—" But she did not finish. She fell back upon her pillows. She had fainted again.

Agnes did not die, nor did her child. She had kept her body clean and healthy. She was up and around again, but an Agnes that never smiled, never chuckled any more. She was a grey pathetic shadow of herself. She who had loved joy so much, cared more, it seemed, for solitude than anything else in the world. That was why, when Jim or I went looking for her we found so often only the empty room and that imperceptibly closing, slowly closing, opposite door.

Joe went back to Mississippi and not one of us, ever again, mentioned Bob's name.

And Jim, poor Jim! I wish I could tell you of how beautiful he was those days. How he never complained, never was irritable, but was always so gentle, so full of understanding, that at times, I had to go out of the room for fear he might see my tears.

Only once I saw him when he thought himself alone. I had not known he was in his little den and entered it suddenly. I had made no sound, luckily, and he had not heard me. He was sitting leaning far forward, his head between his hands. I stood there five minutes at least, but not once did I see him stir. I silently stole out and left him.

It was a fortunate thing that Agnes had already done most of her sewing for the little expected stranger, for after Joe's visit, she never touched a thing.

"Agnes!" I said one day, not without fear and trepidation it is true. "Isn't there something I can do?"

"Do?" she repeated rather vaguely.

"Yes. Some sewing?"

"Oh! sewing," she said. "No, I think not, Lucy."

"You've—you've finished?" I persisted.

"No."

"Then—" I began.

"I hardly think we shall need any of them." And then she added, "I hope not."

"Agnes!" I cried out.

But she seemed to have forgotten me.

Well, time passed, it always does. And on a Sunday morning early Agnes' child was born. He was a beautiful, very grave baby with her great dark eyes.

As soon as they would let me, I went to her.

She was lying very still and straight, in the quiet, darkened room, her head turned on the pillow towards the wall. Her eyes were closed.

"Agnes!" I said in the barest whisper. "Are you asleep?"

"No," she said. And turned her head towards me and opened her eyes. I looked into her ravaged face. Agnes Milton had been down into Hell and back again.

Neither of us spoke for some time and then she said:

"Is he dead?"

"Your child?"

"Yes."

"I should say not, he's a perfect darling and so good."

No smile came into her face. It remained as expressionless as before. She paled a trifle more, I thought, if such a thing was possible.

"I'm sorry," she said finally.

"Agnes!" I spoke sharply. I couldn't help it.

But she closed her eyes and made no response.

I sat a long time looking at her. She must have felt my gaze for she slowly lifted her lids and looked at me.

"Well," she said, "what is it, Lucy?"

"Haven't you seen your child, Agnes?"

"No."

"Don't you wish to see it?"

"No."

Again it was wrung out of me:

"Agnes, Agnes, don't tell me you don't love it."

For the first and only time a spasm of pain went over her poor pinched face.

"Ah!" she said. "That's it." And she closed her eyes and her face was as expressionless as ever.

I felt as though my heart were breaking.

Again she opened her eyes.

"Tell me, Lucy," she began.

"What, Agnes?"

"Is he—healthy?"

"Yes."

"Quite strong?"

"Yes."

"You think he will live, then?"

"Yes, Agnes."

She closed her eyes once more. It was very still within the room.

Again she opened her eyes. There was a strange expression in them now.

"Lucy!"

"Yes."

"You were wrong."

"Wrong, Agnes?"

"Yes."

"How?"

"You thought your God was pitiful."

"Agnes, but I do believe it."

After a long silence she said very slowly:

"He—is—not."

This time, when she closed her eyes, she turned her head slowly upon the pillow to the wall. I was dismissed.

And again Agnes did not die. Time passed and again she was up and about the flat. There was a strange, stony stillness upon her, now, I did not like, though. If we only could have understood, Jim and I, what it meant. Her love for solitude, now, had become a passion. And Jim and I knew more and more that empty room and that silently, slowly closing door.

She would have very little to do with her child. For some reason, I saw, she was afraid of it. I was its mother. I did for it, cared for it, loved it.

Twice only during these days I saw that stony stillness of hers broken.

The first time was one night. The baby was fast asleep, and she had stolen in to look at him, when she thought no one would know. I never wish to see such a tortured, hungry face again.

I was in the kitchen, the second time, when I heard strange sounds coming from my room. I rushed to it and there was Agnes, kneeling at the foot of the little crib, her head upon the spread. Great, terrible racking sobs were tearing her. The baby was lying there, all eyes, and beginning to whimper a little.

"Agnes! Oh, my dear! What is it?" The tears were streaming down my cheeks.

"Take him away! Take him away!" she gasped. "He's

been cooing, and smiling and holding out his little arms to me. I can't stand it! I can't stand it."

I took him away. That was the only time I ever saw Agnes Milton weep.

The baby slept in my room, Agnes would not have him in hers. He was a restless little sleeper and I had to get up several times during the night to see that he was properly covered.

He was a noisy little sleeper as well. Many a night I have lain awake listening to the sound of his breathing. It is a lovely sound, a beautiful one—the breathing of a little baby in the dark.

This night, I remember, I had been up once and covered him over and had fallen off to sleep for the second time, when, for I had heard absolutely no sound, I awoke suddenly. There was upon me an over-whelming utterly paralyzing feeling not of fear but of horror. I thought, at first, I must have been having a nightmare, but strangely instead of diminishing, the longer I lay awake, the more it seemed to increase.

It was a moonlight night and the light came in through the open window in a broad, white, steady stream.

A coldness seemed to settle all about my heart. What was the matter with me? I made a tremendous effort and sat up. Everything seemed peaceful and quiet enough.

The moonlight cut the room in two. It was dark where I was and dark beyond where the baby was.

One brass knob at the foot of my bed shone brilliantly, I remember, in that bright stream and the door that led into the hall stood out fully revealed. I looked at that door and then my heart suddenly seemed to stop beating! I grew deathly cold. The door was closing slowly, inperceptibly, silently. Things were whirling around. I shut my eyes. When I opened them again the door was no longer moving; it had closed.

What had Agnes Milton wanted in my room? And the more I asked myself that question the deeper grew the horror.

And then slowly, by degrees, I began to realize there was something wrong within that room, something terribly wrong. But what was it?

I tried to get out of bed; but I seemed unable to move. I strained my eyes, but I could see nothing—only that bright knob, that stream of light, that closed white door.

I listened. It was quiet, very quiet, too quiet. But why too quiet? And then as though there had been a blinding flash of lightning I knew—the breathing wasn't there.

Agnes Milton had taken a pillow off of my bed and smothered her child.

One last word. Jim received word this morning. The door has finished closing for the last time—Agnes Milton is no more. God, I think, may be pitiful, after all.

First published in the magazine *The Birth Control Review* (Sept–Oct 1919)

GEORGIA DOUGLAS JOHNSON

Motherhood

Don't knock on my door, little child,
I cannot let you in;
You know not what a world this is
Of cruelty and sin.
Wait in the still eternity
Until I come to you.
The world is cruel, cruel, child,
I cannot let you through.

Don't knock at my heart, little one,
I cannot bear the pain
Of turning deaf ears to your call,
Time and time again.
You do not know the monster men
Inhabiting the earth.
Be still, be still, my precious child,
I cannot give you birth.

First published in the magazine
The Crisis (October 1922)

Mizeriah Johnson: Her Arisings and Shinings

Andrew and Maria Johnson, a worthy colored couple living on the outskirts of a large town in Virginia, were the happy possessors of a baby girl. "What shall we name the baby?" had been the subject for discussion in this favored household for some weeks past.

Andrew Johnson came of a family that had "no mush of concession" in its make-up. He was possessed of that order of mind that once an idea had gained a footing in it, the more you argued against it, the more firmly fixed it became. Maria, his wife, was a novice in the art of matrimony and the full force of this fact had not yet dawned upon her, so argue she would and the more she argued a point the more stubborn Andrew became.

Maria had been for several days complaining of a "misery in her side." This complaint she had for two continuous weeks, sandwiched into all matrimonial conversations, along with the query, "What shall we name the baby?" At last Andrew said, jokingly, "I guess I'll name that baby 'Misery' for that pain in your side."

Maria was horror-stricken. At once the argument started and as usual Andrew got "set in the notion," which he bolstered up thus: "That white man that said, 'I wanted my first baby girl named they are always poorly, or so, or middlin', or have a misery in their side, they're never right well' was telling the truth, and Misery that baby shall be named."

Maria cried and protested in vain. She said, "I

wanted my first baby girl named after myself, or rather 'Riah' for short, and 'sides it would sound more stylish," but all to no purpose.

At last the day for the important ceremony arrived and the couple, the baby and the expectant friends, all sallied forth. At the font, Rev. Simon Colfax leaned forward (after taking the baby in his arms) and blandly asked the name. "Misery," said Andrew. "Riah," piped the little mother. The Rev. Simon was a little deaf, and catching a part of each name spoken, leaning forward, murmured questioningly, "Mizeriah?" Now whether the humor of the situation struck Andrew or whether in his heart he relented and determined to yield at last partially to the wishes of the little mother will never be known, but strong and firm came the reply, "Yes Mizeriah," and then came the words, "Mizeriah Johnson, I baptize thee," and the baby was named for good and all Mizeriah Johnson.

Mizeriah was a plump little nut-brown baby and she grew and thrived in spite of her name: all the misery in it never seemed to cause her one moment of trouble. Maria, the mother, used to sit and rock the little brown mite by the hour, singing her favorite hymn, beginning, "Arise and shine." Whether it was the baby's natural bent or whether the little mother sung it into the warp and woof of her spirit, no mortal man can tell, but by the time she could step the little Mizeriah exhibited a ceaseless desire to "rise and shine."

Fond of approbation to a fault she continually brought down wrath upon her small head by the display of these rising and shining qualities. With her head high up in the air, she would pass her parents and humble friends unnoticed. The old folks complained that the little "Mizzy" went by them without even saying "howdy." Her little schoolmates formed rings and sung tauntingly, "Oh, Miss Johnsing turn me loose."

When she had grown a little older and was severely whipped by a larger girl in the schoolyard, "for doin' nuthin'," as she protested, the inquiry developed the fact that Mizzy was supposed to have been "puttin' on airs." "Yes she aired me and I slapped her," was the assailant's explanation of the whole matter.

Another method of making the high-minded little miss miserable, was to ring the changes upon her name in imitation of mother Maria's excited tones. "Mizzy, Mizz-ee, Mizer-iah-Miz-er-riah, Riah, Ri-uh, you Miz-eriah Johnson," until the little girl heartily detested her name.

All of these petty persecutions brought the tears continually to Mizzy's eyes, but did nothing toward curing her of the innate desire to rise and shine. Mizeriah often listened at night to her father arguing dogmatically on various subjects. The last time it had been on what was the most useful, a classical or an industrial education.

Andrew had been on the side of an industrial education. The first fruits of the little girl's listening came forth at the Literary Society where one of the older girls had taken Mizzy as a visitor. The argument started pro and con for industrial or classical education. In a lull of the discussion, Mizeriah took the side of industrial education and gave this illustration against the classical idea, as she had heard her father argue it:

"A woman was drownin' and she called out, sistence, sistence, instid of help, help, and so she got drowned cause the man on the bank didn't have no time to go git a dictionary to see what sistence meant." This unexpected speech from little Mizzy certainly electrified the audience, but it met with instant disapproval. The older and more conservative said Mizzy "was too forrid," and the younger and more radical, that she was "agin the using of big words." The President wishing to remain popular with all, waved his hand to Mizzy to be seated.

The second attempt of Mizzy to shine publicly fared very little better. She slipped off early and went to church during a revival service. The meeting grew enthusiastic and Mizzy determined not to hide her light under a bushel. One of her favorite hymns has a refrain, "Don't call the roll till I get there."

Now Mizzy understood fully the unpleasantness of missing this important ceremony at school. Another hymn recited "Hell is a dark and dismal place," and Mizzy also hated the dark.

Exhortation and song for the moving of sinners' hearts followed one after the other. Then came Mizzy's sweet soprano voice singing the refrain, "Don't call the roll till I get there." Line after line of the hymn was intoned; then came, "Hell is a dark and dismal place." And following it Mizzy again sung, "Don't call the roll till I get there."

A whole bench full of bad boys thereupon got to giggling and sister Martha Saunders marched them ignominiously down the centre aisle and out into the hallway. "Why you all have this way?" was the indignant query. "Mizzy Johnson singed, don't go to the bad place till she git there," was the unexpected reply. Up went sister Martha's hands in holy horror, and down to the parsonage the next morning sallied the good sister, and the pastor was kindly but firmly told, "he must stop Mizzy Johnson sittin' in the Amen corner and leaden hymns."

Our little girl grew somewhat discouraged after this,

and some time had elapsed and the community had ceased to laugh at the little one's attempt to "rise and shine"; but the desire had remained in her heart and had grown with her growth and strengthened with her strength. But now Mizzy had at last finished the grammar school and two years of the High School lay behind under memory's lock and key.

The Woman's Missionary Society held a session during the Annual Conference. Volunteers were called upon to speak and once more Mizzy determined to rise and shine. Upon invitation she rose and spoke on "Answers to prayer." She quoted that story about the little girl who had been disobedient and was sent up stairs by her mother to pray over the matter, and who was not to return until she had received an answer to her prayers. When the mother returned and found the little miss in the parlor enjoying herself, she called her aside and asked, "Have you prayed and was your prayer answered?" "Yes," came the reply. "And what did the Lord say?" "Why he said, 'My Lord Molly, you ain't the wostest child in this whole world; get up and go right down stair.'"

Now this was Mrs. Sadie Jame's pet illustration and she looked daggers at poor Mizzy for usurping her rights.

Next came the invitation for solos. To this request Mizzy also responded by singing the "Last Rose of Summer," and as an encore, "Down on the Swanee River." These were another sister's especially favorite vocal offerings, so she was forced to decline to sing at all. And the spiteful murmur began to circulate, "Mizzy Johnson must be trying to rise and shine with a vengeance tonight."

It was promptly announced that no more invitations

would be issued to volunteers at that session of the conference. But there was a worse fate still in store for these irate and jealous women. They had entirely overlooked the fact that the Sabbath School was to hold its exercises the last evening and that the tableaux might give Mizzy yet another opportunity to show her rising and shining qualities, both to her satisfaction and to their discomfiture. One after the other the tableaux appeared. Some home life, some romantic and others representative of historical groups.

Mizzy had longed for revenge on her jealous associates and she felt that the facts were propitious in the opportunity to appear in these tableaux. She had spent all her small earnings and pocket change for six months on her costume; she had secured, with no difficulty, the handsomest and most popular young man of the congregation to act as the groom, and they had kept their secret well as to the subject of the tableaux they would present that night.

So when the announcement was made the next tableau will be "Coming to the Parson," every neck was craned. Always a popular subject, who would give it tonight, was the query. The curtain rose and there stood Mizzy in her fleecy, fluffy bridal robes; her beautiful sparkling eyes, the wealth of lustrous, rippling waves of hair peeping from beneath the beautiful veil and bridal wreath, her tall, slender, but graceful figure set off to the best advantage by the clinging folds of her dress, and by her side the groom, manly in his bearing, looking pleased with the choice of a partner, if even only for one evening.

Friends and enemies looked with delight on the beautiful picture before them, then came round after round of deafening applause. The curtain rose a second and third time on the tableau, the success of the evening.

Now the young pastor had long secretly admired Mizzy, but had been kept from making his predilection public because of the church sisters' disapproval of Mizzy's rising and shining qualities. But tonight, with heart beating and throbbing so wildly as he looked upon the scene before him, he cast all doubt behind him. His heart so long wavering in allegiance toward these belligerent sisters, now gave the deciding vote against them and entirely in favor of Mizzy.

As the curtain rose a second time he glanced at the groom and as he viewed that gentleman's complacent smile, a great wave of jealousy swept through him. The curtain rose a third time; he could stand it no longer, and slipping inside the curtained enclosure where the performers would soon pass and where Mizzy with her arms laden with flowers soon came gliding swiftly by, he grasped her hands; all the love of his heart was in his eyes; in the tones of his voice. "O, Mizzy, Mizzy, I love you so my darling. Promise to be my wife."

Mizzy glanced up, not so greatly surprised; her woman's heart had discovered his secret long ago and resented his lack of faith in her. For an instant the shapely head tossed coquettishly and the desire to punish for past sins rose strong in her heart and shone forth from her beautiful eyes.

"Oh, Mizzy, promise me won't you? Promise, dear." For an answer, one little brown hand slipped softly into his own broad palm. He looked down again into the sweet eyes and read in their depths that he had won his heart's desire. Before another word could be spoken in drifted all the merry performers in the evening's entertainment, and the lover was forced to be content.

Just then an old classmate of the pastor entered the door. Mizzy's admirer gave her one parting glance and went to greet his friend. In his study he told him gleefully of his matrimonial prospects and dwelt, as all true lovers must, upon the charms of his intended bride. The visiting friend was invited to make a short closing address. While this part of the programme was being carried out the pastor was persuading Mizzy and her parents, Maria and Andrew, to let the tableau, "Coming to the Parson" be repeated as a reality. Mizzy left it all to her parents to decide.

Now Andrew and Maria had all along resented the disposition to flout their little daughter in the church work and fully realized that this ceremony would give complete triumph, so they willingly gave their blessings and consent. Smilingly they took their seats among the congregation. The visiting pastor requested silence and stated that there would now be a marriage ceremony performed. The organ pealed forth its glad notes of the wedding march; the curiosity of the congregation was aroused to its highest pitch; necks were again craned in vain attempts to solve this second mystery of the evening.

At last the door swung open and in came the bridal party; up to the altar they passed and there stood Mizzy Johnson, "coming to the parson" to be made the bride of a parson. All descriptions of silence fail to make clear the complete cessation of noise in that church; not a whisper or a cough; scarcely a breath was drawn while the service was performed.

Then and there Mizzy Johnson had her revenge. She had indeed "arisen and shone." All the years of taunts and persecutions, what were they to her at this moment. They lay behind her and her new found joy.

But the rising and shining of the new bride was of short duration on that charge, for sister Saunders circulated a petition asking for the removal of the young pastor at the close of the conference year.

The Bishop being a diplomat, advised the young brother to make the change, although he had many earnest supporters at his present mission.

When the good Bishop took Mizzy's small hand in his upon her arrival at the new charge and said, "Sister Mizeriah, I hope you may rise and shine in good works, upon this, your new field of labor," a demure smile passed over the countenance of that little lady, but the good Bishop knew not the meaning thereof.

First published in *Colored American Magazine* (Jan–Feb 1902)

CARRIE WILLIAMS CLIFFORD

Negro Players on Broadway

Behold! a Star is trembling in the East,
Whose pale light heralds a triumphant day,
The greatness of whose promise none can say,
Nor who the guest of honor at the feast,
When from the thrall of prejudice released,
Men see the Soul behind the Veil of Clay.
Then brother recognizing brother, may
Divine that least is great and great is least.

A beacon in the wilderness, O Star,
With ox-like eyes we note your lureful gleam.
And Star, so faintly shining from afar,
With God-like faith we watch the widening stream.
Of light! Ho, Christ has come! the perfect day
In glory breaks never to pass away!

First published in Carrie Williams Clifford's
collection The Widening Light (1922)

MARITA BONNER

Nothing New

There was, once high on a hillside, a muddy brook. A brook full of yellow muddy water that foamed and churned over a rock bed.

Halfway down the hillside the water pooled in the clearest pool. All the people wondered how the muddy water cleared at that place. They did not know. They did not understand. They only went to the pool and drank. Sometimes they stooped over and looked into the water and saw themselves.

If they had looked deeper they might have seen God.

People seldom look that deep, though. They do not always understand how to do things.

They are not God. He alone understands.

You have been down on Frye Street. You know how it runs from Grand Avenue and the L to a river; from freckled-faced tow heads to yellow Orientals; from broad Italy to broad Georgia, from hooked nose to square black noses. How it lisps in French, how it babbles in Italian, how it gurgles in German, how it drawls and crawls through Black Belt dialects. Frye Street flows nicely together. It is like muddy water. Like muddy water in a brook.

Reuben Jackson and his wife Bessie—late of Georgia—made a home of three rooms at number thirteen Frye Street.

"Bad luck number," said the neighbors.

"Good luck number," said Reuben and Bessie.

Reuben did not know much. He knew only God, work, church, work and God. The only things Bessie knew were God, work, Denny, prayer, Reuben, prayer, Denny, work, work, work, God.

Denny was one thing they both knew beside God and work. Denny was their little son. He knew lots of things. He knew that when the sun shone across the room a cobwebby shaft appeared that you could not walk up. And when the water dripped on pans in the sink it sang a tune: "Hear the time! Feel the time! Beat with me! Tap-ty tap! T-ta-tap! Ta-ty-tap!" The water sang a tune that made your feet move.

"Stop that jigging, you Denny," Bessie always cried. "God! Don't let him be no dancing man." She would pray afterwards. "Don't let him be no toy-tin fool man!"

Reuben watched him once sitting in his sun shaft. Watched him drape his slender little body along the floor and lift his eyes toward the sunlight. Even then they were eyes that drew deep and told deeper. With his oval clear brown face and his crinkled shining hair, Denny looked too—well as Reuben thought no boy should look. He spoke:

"Why don't you run and wrestle and race with the other boys? You must be a girl. Boys play rough and fight!"

Denny rolled over and looked up at his father. "I ain't a girl!" he declared deliberately.

He started around the room for something to fight to prove his assertion. The cat lay peacefully sleeping by the stove. Denny snatched hold of the cat's tail to awaken it. The cat came up with all claws combing Denny.

"My God, ain't he cruel," screamed his mother. She slapped Denny and the cat apart.

Denny lay down under the iron board and considered the odd red patterns that the claws had made on his arms . . . A red house and a red hill. Red trees around it; a red path running up the hill . . .

"Make my child do what's right," prayed Bessie ironing above him.

People are not God. He alone understands.

Denny was running full tilt down a hillside. Whooping, yelling, shouting. Flying after nothing. Young Frye Street, mixed as usual, raced with him.

There was no school out here. There were no street cars, no houses, no ash-cans and basement stairs to interfere with a run. Out here you could run straight, swift, in one direction with nothing to stop you but your own lack of foot power and breath. A picnic "out of town" pitched your spirits high and Young Frye Street could soar through all twelve heavens of enjoyment.

The racers reached the foot of the hill. Denny swerved to one side. A tiny colored girl was stooping over in the grass.

"Hey, Denny!" she called. Denny stopped to let the others sweep by.

"Hey, Margaret!" he answered. "What you doing?"

Margaret held up a handful of flowers. "I want that one." She pointed to a clump of dusky purple milkweeds bending behind a bush.

Denny hopped toward it.

He had almost reached it when the bush parted and a boy stepped out: "Don't come over here," he ordered. "This is the white kids' side!"

Denny looked at him. He was not of Frye Street.

Other strange children appeared behind him. "This is a white picnic over here! Stay away from our side."

Denny continued toward his flower. Margaret squatted contentedly in the grass. She was going to get her flower.

"I said not to come over here," yelled the boy behind the bush.

Denny hopped around the bush.

"What you want over here?" the other bristled.

"That flower!" Denny pointed.

The other curved his body out in exaggerated childish sarcasm. "Sissy! Picking flowers." He turned to the boys behind him. "Sissy nigger! Picking flowers!"

Denny punched at the boy and snatched at the flower. The other stuck out his foot and Denny dragged him down as he fell. Young Frye Street rushed back up the hill at the primeval howl that set in.

Down on the ground, Denny and the white boy squirmed and kicked. They dug and pounded each other.

"You stay off the white kids' side, nigger!"

"I'm going to get that flower, I am!" Denny dragged his enemy along with him as he lunged toward the bush.

The flower beckoned and bent its stalk. On the white kids' side. Lovely, dusky, purple. Bending toward him. The milky perfume almost reached him. On the white kids' side. He wanted it. He would get it. Something ripped.

Denny left the collar of his blouse in the boy's hand and wrenched loose. He grabbed at the stem. On the white kids' side. Bending to him—slender, bending to him. On the white kids' side. He wanted it. He was going to have it—

The boy caught up to him as he had almost reached the flower. They fell again.—He was going to get that flower. He was going to. Tear the white kid off. Tear the white hands off his throat. Tear the white kid off his arms. Tear the white kid's weight off his chest. He'd move him—

Denny made a twist and slid low to the ground, the other boy beneath him, face downward. He pinned the boy's shoulders to the ground and clutching a handful of blonde hair in either hand, beat his head against the ground.

Young Frye Street sang the song of triumph. Sang it long and loud. Sang it loud enough for Mrs. Bessie Jackson—resting under a clump of trees with other mothers—to hear.

"I know them children is fighting!" she declared and started off in the direction of the yelling.

Halfway she met Margaret, a long milkweed flower dragging in one hand: "Denny," she explained, holding it up.

"I knew it," cried his mother and ran the rest of the way. "Stop killing that child," she screamed as soon as she had neared the mob. She dragged Denny off the boy. Dragged him through the crowd under the tree. Then she began:

"Look at them clothes. Where is your collar at? All I do is try to fix you up and now look at you! Look at you! Even your shirt torn!"

"Just as well him tear that for what he said," Denny offered.

This approximated "sauce" or the last straw or the point of overflow. His mother was staggered. Was there nothing she could do? Unconsciously she looked up to

Heaven, then down to earth. A convenient bush flaunted nearby. She pulled it up—by the roots.

—On the white kids' side. The flower he wanted.—

God understands, doesn't He?

It had been a hard struggle. Reuben was still bitter and stubborn:

"What reason Denny got to go to some art school? What he going to learn there?"

"Art! Painting!" Bessie defended. "The teachers at the high school say he know how to paint special like. He'd ought to go, they said."

"Yes, they said, but they ain't going to pay for him. He ought to go somewhere and do some real man's work. Ain't nothin' but women paddlin' up and down, worryin' about paintin'."

"He's going all the same. Them teachers said he was better—!"

"Oh, all right. Let him go."

And Denny went to the Littler Art School. Carried his joyous six-foot, slender, brown self up on Grand Avenue, across, under, the elevated towers—up town. Up town to school.

"Bessie Jackson better put him on a truck like Annie Turner done her Jake," declared colored Frye Street. "Ain't no man got no business spendin' his life learnin' to paint."

"He should earn money! Money!" protested one portion of Frye Street through its hooked noses.

"Let him marry a wife," chuckled the Italians.

"He's going to learn art," said Denny's mother.

Denny went. The Littler School was filled with students of both sexes and of all races and degrees of life. Most of them were sufficiently gifted to be there. Days there when they showed promise. Days there when they doubted their own reasons for coming.

Denny did as well and as badly as the rest. Sometimes he even did things that attracted attention.

He himself always drew attention, for he was tall, straight and had features that were meant to go with the blondest hair and the bluest eyes. He was not blond though. He was clean shaven and curly haired and brown as any Polynesian. His eyes were still deep drawing—deep telling. Eyes like a sea-going liner that could drift far without getting lost; that could draw deep without sinking.

Some women scrambled to make an impression on him. If they had looked at his mouth they would have withheld their efforts.

Anne Forest was one of the scramblers. She did not know she was scrambling, though. If anyone had told her that she was, she would have exploded, "Why! He is a nigger!"

Anne, you see, was white. She was the kind of girl who made you feel that she thrived on thirty-nine cent chocolates, fifteen-dollar silk dress sales, twenty-five cent love stories and much guilty smootchy kissing. If that does not make you sense her water-waved bob, her too carefully rouged face, her too perfumed person, I cannot bring her any nearer to you.

Anne scrambled unconsciously. Denny was an attractive man. Denny knew she was scrambling—so he went further within himself.

Went so far within himself that he did not notice Pauline Hammond who sat next to him.

One day he was mixing paint in a little white dish. Somehow the dish capsized and the paint flowed over the desk and spattered.

"Oh, my heavens!" said a girl's voice.

Denny stood up: "I beg your pardon." He looked across the desk.

Purple paint was splashed along the girl's smock and was even on her shoes.

"Oh, that's all right! No harm done at all," she said pleasantly.

Nice voice. Not jagged or dangling. Denny looked at her again. He dipped his handkerchief into the water and wiped off the shoes.

That done, they sat back and talked to each other. Talked to each other that day and the next day. Several days they talked.

Denny began to notice Pauline carefully. She did not talk to people as if they were strange hard shells she had to crack open to get inside. She talked as if she were already in the shell. In their very shell.

—Not many people can talk that soul-satisfying way. Why? I do not know. I am not God. I do not always understand—.

They talked about work; their life outside of school. Life. Life out in the world. With an artist's eye Denny noted her as she talked. Slender, more figure than heavy form, molded. Poised. Head erect on neck, neck uplifted on shoulders, body held neither too stiff nor too slack. Poised and slenderly molded as an aristocrat.

They thought together and worked together. Saw things through each other's eyes. They loved each other.

One day they went to a Sargent exhibit—and saw Anne Forest. She gushed and mumbled and declared war on Pauline. She did not know she had declared war, though.

"Pauline Hammond goes out with that nigger Denny Jackson!" she informed all the girls in class the next day.

"With a nigger!" The news seeped through the school. Seeped from the President's office on the third floor to the janitor down below the stairs.

Anne Forest only told one man the news. He was Allen Carter. He had taken Pauline to three dances and Anne to one. Maybe Anne was trying to even the ratio when she told him: "Pauline Hammond is rushing a nigger now."

Allen truly reeled. "Pauline! A nigger?"

Anne nodded. "Denny Jackson—or whatever his name is," she hastened to correct herself.

Allen cursed aloud. "Pauline! She's got too much sense for that! It's that nigger rushing after her! Poor little kid! I'll kill him!"

He tore off his smock with a cursing accompaniment. He cursed before Anne. She did not matter. She should have known that before.

Allen tore off the smock and tore along the hall. Tore into a group gathered in a corner bent over a glass case. Denny and Pauline were in the crowd, side by side. Allen walked up to Denny.

"Here you," he pushed his way in between the two. "Let this white girl alone." He struck Denny full in the face.

Denny struck back. All the women—except Pauline—fled to the far end of the room.

The two men fought. Two jungle beasts would have been kinder to each other. These two tore at each other with more than themselves behind every blow.

"Let that white woman alone, nigger! Stay on your own side!" Allen shouted once.—On your own side. On the white kids' side. That old fight—the flower, bending toward him. He'd move the white kid! Move him and get the flower! Move him and get what was his! He

133

seized a white throat in his hands and moved his hands close together!

He did move the white kid. Moved him so completely that doctors and running and wailing could not cause his body to stir again. Moved him so far that Denny was moved to the County Jail.

Everything moved then. The judge moved the jury with pleas to see justice done for a man who had sacrificed his life for the beautiful and the true. The jury moved that the old law held: one life taken, take another.

Denny—they took Denny.

Up at the school the trustees moved. "Be it enacted this day—no Negro student shall enter within these doors—."

The newspapers moved their readers. Sent columns of description of the "hypnotized frail flower under the spell of Black Art." So completely under the spell she had to be taken from the stand for merely screaming in the judge's face: "I loved him! I loved him! I loved him!" until the court ran over with the cries.

Frye Street agreed on one thing only. Bessie and Reuben had tried to raise Denny right.

After that point, Frye Street unmixed itself. Flowed apart.

Frye Street—black—was loud in its utterances. "Served Denny right for loving a white woman! Many white niggers as there is! Either Bessie or Reuben must have loved white themselves and was 'shamed to go out open with them. Shame to have that all come out in that child! Now he rottenin' in a murderer's grave!"

White Frye Street held it was the school that had ruined Denny. Had not Frye Street—black and white—played together, worked together, shot crap together, fought together without killing? When a nigger got in school he got crazy.

Up on the hillside the clear water pooled. Up on the hillside people come to drink at the pool. If they looked over, they saw themselves. If they had looked deeper— deeper than themselves—they might have seen God.

But they did not.

People do not do that—do they?

They do not always understand. Do they?

God alone—He understands.

First published in the magazine
The Crisis (November 1926)

CLARA ANN THOMPSON

Mrs. Johnson Objects

Come right in this house, Will Johnson!
 Kin I teach you dignity?
Chasin' aft' them po' white children,
 Jest because you wan'to play.

Whut does po' white trash keer fah you?
 Want you keep away fum them,
Next, they'll be a-doin' meanness,
 An' a-givin' you the blame.

Don't come mumblin' 'bout their playthings,
 Yourn is good enough fah you;
'Twus the best that I could git you,
 An' you've got to make them do,

Go'n' to break you fum that habit,
 Yes, I am! An' mighty soon,
Next, you'll grow up like the white-folks,
 All time whinin' fah the moon.

Runnin' with them po' white children—
 Go'n' to break it up, I say!—
Pickin' up their triflin' habits,
 Soon, you'll be as spilte as they.

Come on here, an' take the baby—
 Mind now! Don't you let her fall—
'Fo' I'll have you runnin' with them,
 I won't let you play at all.

Jest set there, an' mind the baby
    Till I tell you—You may go;
An' jest let me ketch you chasin'
    Aft' them white trash any mo'.

First published in Clara Ann Thompson's
collection *Songs from the Wayside* (1908)

Son

We wandered through the meadow, green and cool,
My romping, joyous little son and I.
Bright was the rippling stream and we, withal,
So gay, we noted not the flying hours
'Til suddenly the sun had set, and gray,
Dim shadows o'er the earth began to creep.

No longer now he sang in childish glee,
Or sought the modest flower in cranny hid;
But close beside me walked in sober mood,
His hand close-clasped in mine; then coaxingly,
" 'Tis dark, dear father; please, sir, take me home!"

My little son to manhood now has grown;
No longer fears he shadows dim and gray;
In fearlessness of youth, he braves the dark,
But I, who know the dangers of the dark
And all the ills which do in darkness lurk,

Am fearful, lest he stumble and so fall
Into the pit: but when Life's Day is done,
When burst all the bubbles he has chased,
And creeping come the shadows of the night,
Do Thou, dear Father, hold his trembling hand
And through the darkness lead him gently Home.

First published in Carrie Williams Clifford's
collection *The Widening Light* (1922)

ALICE DUNBAR-NELSON

A Carnival Jangle

There is a merry jangle of bells in the air, an all-pervading sense of jester's noise, and the flaunting vividness of royal colours. The streets swarm with humanity,—humanity in all shapes, manners, forms, laughing, pushing, jostling, crowding, a mass of men and women and children, as varied and assorted in their several individual peculiarities as ever a crowd that gathered in one locality since the days of Babel.

It is Carnival in New Orleans; a brilliant Tuesday in February, when the very air gives forth an ozone intensely exhilarating, making one long to cut capers. The buildings are a blazing mass of royal purple and golden yellow, national flags, bunting, and decorations that laugh in the glint of the Midas sun. The streets are a crush of jesters and maskers, Jim Crows and clowns, ballet girls and Mephistos, Indians and monkeys; of wild and sudden flashes of music, of glittering pageants and comic ones, of befeathered and belled horses; a dream of colour and melody and fantasy gone wild in an effervescent bubble of beauty that shifts and changes and passes kaleidoscope-like before the bewildered eye.

A bevy of bright-eyed girls and boys of that uncertain age that hovers between childhood and maturity, were moving down Canal Street when there was a sudden jostle with another crowd meeting them. For a minute there was a deafening clamour of shouts and laughter, cracking of the whips, which all maskers carry, a jingle and clatter of carnival bells, and the masked and unmasked extricated themselves and moved from each other's paths. But in the confusion a tall Prince of Darkness had whispered to one of the girls in the unmasked crowd: "You'd better come with us, Flo; you're wasting time in that tame gang. Slip off, they'll never miss you; we'll get you a rig, and show you what life is."

And so it happened, when a half-hour passed, and the bright-eyed bevy missed Flo and couldn't find her, wisely giving up the search at last, she, the quietest and most bashful of the lot, was being initiated into the mysteries of "what life is."

Down Bourbon Street and on Toulouse and St. Peter Streets there are quaint little old-world places where one may be disguised effectually for a tiny consideration. Thither, guided by the shapely Mephisto and guarded by the team of jockeys and ballet girls, tripped Flo. Into one of the lowest-ceiled, dingiest, and most ancient-looking of these shops they stepped.

"A disguise for the demoiselle," announced Mephisto to the woman who met them. She was small and wizened and old, with yellow, flabby jaws, a neck like the throat of an alligator, and straight, white hair that stood from her head uncannily stiff.

"But the demoiselle wishes to appear a boy, un petit garçon?" she inquired, gazing eagerly at Flo's long, slender frame. Her voice was old and thin, like the high quavering of an imperfect tuning-fork, and her eyes were sharp as talons in their grasping glance.

"Mademoiselle does not wish such a costume," gruffly responded Mephisto.

"Ma foi, there is no other," said the ancient, shrugging her shoulders. "But one is left now; mademoiselle would make a fine troubadour."

"Flo," said Mephisto, "it's a daredevil scheme, try it; no one will ever know it but us, and we'll die before we tell. Besides, we must; it's late, and you couldn't find your crowd."

And that was why you might have seen a Mephisto and a slender troubadour of lovely form, with mandolin flung across his shoulder, followed by a bevy of jockeys and ballet girls, laughing and singing as they swept down Rampart Street.

When the flash and glare and brilliancy of Canal Street have palled upon the tired eye, when it is yet too soon to go home to such a prosaic thing as dinner, and one still wishes for novelty, then it is wise to go into the lower districts. There is fantasy and fancy and grotesqueness run wild in the costuming and the behaviour of the maskers. Such dances and whoops and leaps as these hideous Indians and devils do indulge in; such wild curvetings and long walks! In the open squares, where whole groups do congregate, it is wonderfully amusing. Then, too, there is a ball in every available hall, a delirious ball, where one may dance all day for ten cents; dance and grow mad for joy, and never know who were your companions, and be yourself unknown. And in the exhilaration of the day, one walks miles and miles, and dances and skips, and the fatigue is never felt.

In Washington Square, away down where Royal Street empties its stream of children great and small into the broad channel of Elysian Fields Avenue, there was a perfect Indian pow-wow. With a little imagination one might have willed away the vision of the surrounding houses, and fancied one's self again in the forest, where the natives were holding a sacrediot. The square was filled with spectators, masked and unmasked. It was amusing to watch these mimic Red-men, they seemed so fierce and earnest.

Suddenly one chief touched another on the elbow. "See that Mephisto and troubadour over there?" he whispered huskily.

"Yes; who are they?"

"I don't know the devil," responded the other, quietly, "but I'd know that other form anywhere. It's Leon, see? I know those white hands like a woman's and that restless head. Ha!"

"But there may be a mistake."

"No. I'd know that one anywhere; I feel it is he. I'll pay him now. Ah, sweetheart, you've waited long, but you shall feast now!" He was caressing something long and lithe and glittering beneath his blanket.

In a masked dance it is easy to give a death-blow between the shoulders. Two crowds meet and laugh and shout and mingle almost inextricably, and if a shriek of pain should arise, it is not noticed in the din, and when they part, if one should stagger and fall bleeding to the ground, can any one tell who has given the blow? There is nothing but an unknown stiletto on the ground, the crowd has dispersed, and masks tell no tales anyway. There is murder, but by whom? for what? *Quien sabe?*

And that is how it happened on Carnival night, in the last mad moments of Rex's reign, a broken-hearted mother sat gazing wide-eyed and mute at a horrible something that lay across the bed. Outside the long sweet march music of many bands floated in as if in mockery, and the flash of rockets and Bengal lights illumined the dead, white face of the girl troubadour.

First published in Alice Dunbar-Nelson's collection *The Goodness of St Rocque and Other Stories* (1899)

OLIVIA WARD BUSH-BANKS

Regret

I said a thoughtless word one day,
A loved one heard and went away;
I cried: "Forgive me, I was blind;
I would not wound or be unkind."
I waited long, but all in vain,
To win my loved one back again.
Too late, alas! to weep and pray,
Death came; my loved one passed away.
Then, what a bitter fate was mine;
No language could my grief define;
Tears of deep regret could not unsay
The thoughtless word I spoke that day.

First published in Olivia Ward
Bush-Banks's collection
Driftwood (1914)

GEORGIA DOUGLAS JOHNSON

Escape

Shadows, shadows,
Hug me round
So that I shall not be found
By sorrow;
She pursues me
Everywhere,
I can't lose her
Anywhere.

Fold me in your black
Abyss;
She will never look
In this,—
Shadows, shadows,
Hug me round
In your solitude
Profound.

First published in *The New Negro*, an anthology edited by Alain Locke (1925)

Sanctuary

I

On the Southern coast, between Merton and Shawboro, there is a strip of desolation some half a mile wide
and nearly ten miles long between the sea and old fields
of ruined plantations. Skirting the edge of this narrow
jungle is a partly grown-over road which still shows
traces of furrows made by the wheels of wagons that
have long since rotted away or been cut into firewood.
This road is little used, now that the state has built its
new highway a bit to the west and wagons are less
numerous than automobiles.

In the forsaken road a man was walking swiftly. But
in spite of his hurry, at every step he set down his feet
with infinite care, for the night was windless and the
heavy silence intensified each sound; even the breaking
of a twig could be plainly heard. And the man had need
of caution as well as haste.

Before a lonely cottage that shrank timidly back from
the road the man hesitated a moment, then struck out
across the patch of green in front of it. Stepping behind
a clump of bushes close to the house, he looked in
through the lighted window at Annie Poole, standing at
her kitchen table mixing the supper biscuits.

He was a big, black man with pale brown eyes in
which there was an odd mixture of fear and amazement. The light showed streaks of gray soil on his

heavy, sweating face and great hands, and on his torn clothes. In his woolly hair clung bits of dried leaves and dead grass.

He made a gesture as if to tap on the window, but turned away to the door instead. Without knocking he opened it and went in.

II

The woman's brown gaze was immediately on him, though she did not move. She said, "You ain't in no hurry, is you, Jim Hammer?" It wasn't, however, entirely a question.

"Ah's in trubble, Mis' Poole," the man explained, his voice shaking, his fingers twitching.

"W'at you done done now?"

"Shot a man, Mis' Poole."

"Trufe?" The woman seemed calm. But the word was spat out.

"Yas'm. Shot'im." In the man's tone was something of wonder, as if he himself could not quite believe that he had really done this thing which he affirmed.

"Daid?"

"Dunno, Mis' Poole. Dunno."

"White man o' niggah?"

"Cain't say, Mis' Poole. White man, Ah reckons."

Annie Poole looked at him with cold contempt. She was a tiny, withered woman—fifty perhaps—with a wrinkled face the color of old copper, framed by a crinkly mass of white hair. But about her small figure was some quality of hardness that belied her appearance of frailty. At last she spoke, boring her sharp little eyes into those of the anxious creature before her.

146

"An' w'at am you lookin' foh me to do 'bout et?"

"Jes' lemme stop till dey's gone by. Hide me till dey passes. Reckon dey ain't fur off now." His begging voice changed to a frightened whimper. "Foh de Lawd's sake, Mis' Poole, lemme stop."

And why, the woman inquired caustically, should she run the dangerous risk of hiding him?

"Obadiah, he'd lemme stop ef he was home," the man whined.

Annie Poole sighed. "Yas," she admitted, slowly, reluctantly, "Ah spec' he would. Obadiah, he's too good to youall no 'count trash." Her slight shoulders lifted in a hopeless shrug. "Yas, Ah reckon he'd do et. Emspecial' seein' how he allus set such a heap o' store by you. Cain't see w'at foh, mahse'f. Ah shuah don' see nuffin' in you but a heap o' dirt."

But a look of irony, of cunning, of complicity passed over her face. She went on, "Still, 'siderin' all an' all, how Obadiah's right fon' o' you, an' how white folks is white folks, Ah'm a-gwine hide you dis one time."

Crossing the kitchen, she opened a door leading into a small bedroom, saying, "Git yo'se'f in dat dere feather baid an' Ah'm a-gwine put de clo's on de top. Don' reckon dey'll fin' you ef dey does look foh you in mah house. An Ah don' spec' dey'll go foh to do dat. Not lessen you been keerless an' let 'em smell you out gittin' hyah." She turned on him a withering look. "But you allus been triflin'. Cain't do nuffin' propah. An' Ah'm a-tellin' you ef dey warn't white folks an' you a po' niggah, Ah shuah wouldn't be lettin' you mess up mah feather baid dis ebenin', 'cose Ah jes' plain don' want you hyah. Ah done kep' mahse'f outen trubble all mah life. So's Obadiah."

"Ah's powahful 'bliged to you, Mis' Poole. You shuah am one good 'oman. De Lawd'll mos' suttinly—"

Annie Poole cut him off. "Dis ain't no time foh all dat kin' o' fiddle-de-roll. Ah does mah duty as Ah sees et 'thout no thanks from you. Ef de Lawd had gib you a white face 'stead o' dat dere black one, Ah shuah would turn you out. Now hush yo' mouf an' git you'se'f in. An' don' git movin' and scrunchin' undah dose covahs and git yo'se'f kotched in mah house."

Without further comment the man did as he was told. After he had laid his soiled body and grimy garments between her snowy sheets, Annie Poole carefully rearranged the covering and placed piles of freshly laundered linen on top. Then she gave a pat here and there, eyed the result, and finding it satisfactory, went back to her cooking.

III

Jim Hammer settled down to the racking business of waiting until the approaching danger should have passed him by. Soon savory odors seeped in to him and he realized that he was hungry. He wished that Annie Poole would bring him something to eat. Just one biscuit. But she wouldn't he knew. Not she. She was a hard one, Obadiah's mother.

By and by he fell into a sleep from which he was dragged back by the rumbling sound of wheels in the road outside. For a second fear clutched so tightly at him that he almost leaped from the suffocating shelter of the bed in order to make some active attempt to escape the horror that his capture meant. There was a spasm at his heart, a pain so sharp, so slashing that he had to suppress an impulse to cry out. He felt himself falling. Down, down, down . . . Everything grew dim and very distant in his memory . . . Vanished . . . Came rushing back.

Outside there was silence. He strained his ears. Nothing. No footsteps. No voices. They had gone on then. Gone without even stopping to ask Annie Poole if she had seen him pass that way. A sigh of relief slipped from him. His thick lips curled in an ugly, cunning smile. It had been smart of him to think of coming to Obadiah's mother's to hide. She was an old demon, but he was safe in her house.

He lay a short while longer listening intently, and, hearing nothing, started to get up. But immediately he stopped, his yellow eyes glowing like pale flames. He had heard the unmistakable sound of men coming toward the house. Swiftly he slid back into the heavy hot stuffiness of the bed and lay listening fearfully.

The terrifying sounds drew nearer. Slowly. Heavily. Just for a moment he thought they were not coming in—they took so long. But there was a light knock and the noise of a door being opened. His whole body went taut. His feet felt frozen, his hands clammy, his tongue like a weighted, dying thing. His pounding heart made it hard for his straining ears to hear what they were saying out there.

"Ebenin', Mistah Lowndes." Annie Poole's voice sounded as it always did, sharp and dry.

There was no answer. Or had he missed it? With slow care he shifted his position, bringing his head nearer the edge of the bed. Still he heard nothing. What were they waiting for? Why didn't they ask about him?

Annie Poole, it seemed, was of the same mind. "Ah

149

don' reckon youall done traipsed way out hyah jes' foh yo' healf," she hinted.

"There's bad news for you, Annie, I'm 'fraid." The sheriff's voice was low and queer.

Jim Hammer visualized him standing out there—a tall, stooped man, his white tobacco-stained mustache drooping limply at the ends, his nose hooked and sharp, his eyes blue and cold. Bill Lowndes was a hard one too. And white.

"W'atall bad news, Mistah Lowndes?" The woman put the question quietly, directly.

"Obadiah—" the sheriff began—hesitated—began again. "Obadiah—ah—er—he's outside, Annie. I'm 'fraid—"

"Shucks! You done missed. Obadiah, he ain't done nuffin', Mistah Lowndes. Obadiah!" she called stridently, "Obadiah! git hyah an' splain yose'f."

But Obadiah didn't answer, didn't come in. Other men came in. Came in with steps that dragged and halted. No one spoke. Not even Annie Poole. Something was laid carefully upon the floor.

"Obadiah, chile," his mother said softly, "Obadiah, chile." Then, with sudden alarm, "He ain't daid, is he? Mistah Lowndes! Obadiah, he ain't daid?"

Jim Hammer didn't catch the answer to that pleading question. A new fear was stealing over him.

"There was a to-do, Annie," Bill Lowndes explained gently, "at the garage back o' the factory. Fellow tryin' to steal tires. Obadiah heerd a noise an' run out with two or three others. Scared the rascal all right. Fired off his gun an' run. We allow et to be Jim Hammer. Picked up his cap back there. Never was no 'count. Thievin' an' sly. But we'll git 'im, Annie. We'll git 'im."

The man huddled in the feather bed prayed silently.

"Oh, Lawd! Ah didn't go to do et. Not Obadiah, Lawd. You knows dat. You knows et." And into his frenzied brain came the thought that it would be better for him to get up and go out to them before Annie Poole gave him away. For he was lost now. With all his great strength he tried to get himself out of the bed. But he couldn't.

"Oh Lawd!" he moaned. "Oh Lawd!" His thoughts were bitter and they ran through his mind like panic. He knew that it had come to pass as it said somewhere in the Bible about the wicked. The Lord had stretched out his hand and smitten him. He was paralyzed. He couldn't move hand or foot. He moaned again. It was all there was left for him to do. For in the terror of this new calamity that had come upon him he had forgotten the waiting danger which was so near out there in the kitchen.

His hunters, however, didn't hear him. Bill Lowndes was saying, "We been a-lookin' for Jim out along the old road. Figured he'd make tracks for Shawboro. You ain't noticed anybody pass this evenin', Annie?"

The reply came promptly, unwaveringly. "No, Ah ain't seen nobody pass. Not yet."

IV

Jim Hammer caught his breath.

"Well," the sheriff concluded, "we'll be gittin' along. Obadiah was a mighty fine boy. Ef they was all like him—. I'm sorry, Annie. Anything I c'n do, let me know."

"Thank you, Mistah Lowndes."

With the sound of the door closing on the departing

men, power to move came back to the man in the bed-room. He pushed his dirt-caked feet out from the covers and rose up, but crouched down again. He wasn't cold now, but hot all over and burning. Almost he wished that Bill Lowndes and his men had taken him with them.

Annie Poole had come into the room.

It seemed a long time before Obadiah's mother spoke. When she did there were no tears, no reproaches; but there was a raging fury in her voice as she lashed out, "Git outen mah feather baid, Jim Hammer, an' outen mah house, an' don' nevah stop thankin' yo' Jesus he done gib you dat black face."

First published in the magazine
Forum (January 1930)

LEILA AMOS PENDLETON

An Apostrophe to the Lynched

Hang there, O my murdered brothers, sons of Ethiopia, our common Mother! Hang there, with faces upturned, mutely calling down vengeance from the Most High God!

Call down vengeance upon this barbarous nation; a nation of hypocrites, timeservers and gold-worshippers; a nation of ranting, ramping, stamping creatures who call themselves evangelists and who practice the evangel of restriction and proscription; a nation of wolves who hunt in packs and who skulk away if caught alone; a nation always ready to "avenge" itself against the weak, but with mouth filled with ready excuses for not attacking the strong.

Hang there until their eyes are unsealed and they behold themselves as they are and as they appear to an amazed world! Hang there until their ears are opened to the ominous sounds of warning! Hang there until their foresworn souls perceive the true meaning of Liberty and Justice, until they catch a glimmer of the meaning of Christianity!

Martyrs to lawlessness, bigotry, prejudice, if you by dying can accomplish some of these things, Death will have been swallowed up in Victory.

First published in the magazine
The Crisis (June 1916)

CARRIE WILLIAMS CLIFFORD

We'll Die for Liberty

We are children of oppression who are struggling to
    be free
From injustice, and the galling yoke of color-tyranny;
Our small band is facing bravely a relentless enemy.
      But we go fighting on.

For liberty we'll bare our breasts, and this our cry
    shall be:
"Equal rights and equal justice, equal opportunity."
Undaunted we will face the foe and fight right
    valiantly
      To victory marching on.

In the name of Christ our Lord who suffered death
    upon the tree.
And of the Constitution, our proud country's
    guarantee.
And of the flag which over all should wave
    protectingly
      We'll strike for liberty.

Thus strongly fortified in right we'll strive
    triumphantly.
Till the glorious light of Freedom's torch shall flame
    from sea to sea;
And all the children of our land shall dwell in amity,
      As Truth goes marching on.

Then list, ye Sons of Morning, to a weaker brother's
    plea,
And harken, Hosts of Darkness, to our Heaven-
    inspired decree:
As He died to make men holy we will die for liberty,
    Thou, God, the issue keep.

       Chorus: Glory, glory, hallelujah! | |
           We'll die for liberty!
               | | Repeat three times.

First published in Carrie Williams
Clifford's collection *Race Rhymes* (1911)

CARRIE WILLIAMS CLIFFORD

Silent Protest Parade

(ON FIFTH AVENUE, NEW YORK,
SATURDAY, JULY 28, 1917, PROTESTING
AGAINST THE ST. LOUIS RIOTS)

Were you there? Did you see? Gods! wasn't it fine!
Did you notice how straight we kept the line,
As we marched down the famous avenue,
Silent, dogged and dusky of hue,
Keeping step to the sound of the muffled drum,
With its constantly recurring *tum—tum, tum—*
Tum—Tum—Tum—Tum—Tum;
Ten thousand of us, if there was one!
As goodly a sight as this ancient sun
Has ever looked upon!

Youth and maid
Father, mother—not one afraid
Or ashamed to let the whole world know
What he thought of the hellish East St. Louis "show,"
Orgy—riot—mob—what you will,
Where men and e'en women struggled to kill
Poor black workers, who'd fled in distress from the
    South
To find themselves murdered and mobbed in the
    North.

We marched as a protest—we carried our banner,
On which had been boldly inscribed every manner
    Of sentiment—all, to be sure, within reason—

But no flag—not that we meant any treason—
Only who'd have the heart to carry Old Glory,
After hearing all of the horrible story,
Of East St. Louis? and never a word,
From the nation's head, as if he'd not heard
The groans of the dying ones here at home,
Though 'tis plain he can hear even farther than
      Rome.

Oh, yes, I was there in the Silent Parade,
And a man (he was white) I heard when he said,
"If they had music now, 'twould be great!"—
"We march not, sir, with hearts elate,
But sad; we grieve for our dark brothers
Murdered, and we hope that others
Will heed our protest against wrong,
Will help to make our protest strong."

Were you there? Ah, brothers, wasn't it fine!
The children—God bless 'em—headed the line;
Then came the mothers dressed in white,
And some—my word! 'twas a thrilling sight—
Carried their babies upon their breast,
Face tense and eager as forward they pressed,
With never a laugh and never a word,
But ever and always, the thing they heard
Was the *tum—tum—*, *tum, tum,*
Of the muffled drum—*tum, tum, tum!*

And last the black-coated men swung by,
Head up, chest firm, determined eye—
I was so happy, I wanted to cry.
As I watched the long lines striding by,
(Ten thousand souls if there was one)

And I knew that "to turn, the worm had begun,"
As we marched down Fifth Avenue unafraid
And calm, in our first Silent Protest Parade!

First published in Carrie Williams Clifford's
collection *The Widening Light* (1922)

Eloise Bibb Thompson

Mademoiselle 'Tasie

It was all on account of that last Mardi Gras Ball. Mlle. 'Tasie felt it. Indeed she was absolutely sure of it. The night had been cold and damp and she had not had a wrap suited for such weather. So she had gone in a thin blue organdy dress, the best she owned, with simply a white scarf thrown over her shoulders. A "white" scarf, and a "blue" organdy. It was scandalous! And her "tante" but one year dead. No wonder bad luck in the shape of ill health had followed her ever since—putting off her mourning so soon to go to a Mardi Gras ball. Well, what was the use of thinking of it now? "De milk has been speel, so to speak," she mused, "eet ees a grat wonder, yes, as de doctah say, I deed not go into decline."

But try as she would Mlle. 'Tasie could not stop thinking of it. The heavy cold caught at that Mardi Gras ball was the direct cause of her being about to take the momentous step that she was planning to take to-day. And momentous it was, for a fact; there was not the slightest doubt about that. How it would all end, she was at a loss to comprehend.

Not that it counted so much with her now; for ill health and deprivation had forced her to accept with resignation many things that before had seemed unendurable. But her neighbors, ah! and her relatives who knew how thoroughly she had formerly hated the very thing that she was about to do. Mon Dieu! What were they not saying of her now?

Yes, there was a time in her life when Mlle. 'Tasie would rather have fainted, actually, than to even so much as have been seen on the street with a certain kind of individual, which she and her class designated as a "Negre Americain aux grosses oreilles"—an American Negro with large ears. In a word, with a black American. How many times had she not said of such a contingency, "h-eet h-ees a thing not to be thought h-of h-at h-all." And now—O, now see what she was fixing to do!

For Mlle. 'Tasie was a Creole lady of much less color than a black American. Be pleased to know first of all, that there are colored Creoles as well as white Creoles, just as there are Creole eggs and Creole cabbages. Any person or article brought up in the French Quarter of old New Orleans, the downtown section across Canal Street, is strictly Creole. And to carry the thought to its final conclusion is, in the highest sense of the word, Superior. Mlle. 'Tasie was what was designated by her lightly colored contemporaries, in a whisper, as "un briquet," that is, she had a reddish yellow complexion, and very crinkled red hair. "In a whisper," because the hair of a "briquet" is usually so short and so crinkled that no one feels flattered at being called one. Yet in spite of all that, Mlle. 'Tasie was a Creole, came of a good family, and spoke "patois French" for the most part, sometimes English, and hence, thinking herself superior, had not mingled with English-speaking Negroes known as Americans. And being yellow, she had never been accustomed, until now, to even be on speaking terms with blacks.

It was a positive fact, Mlle. 'Tasie had come of an exceptional Creole family. Everyone with whom she came in contact knew that well. How could they help knowing it when they had heard it so often? As for the corner grocer from whom Mlle. 'Tasie bought charcoal for her diminutive furnace—she couldn't afford a stove—and various other sundries for her almost empty larder, why, had you awakened him from the soundest sort of sleep, he could have told you about her family, word for word, as she had told it, embellished it with glowing incidents, as she had done. In a word, he could have torn that family tree to pieces for you, from root to apex at the shortest possible notice. That was because, of course, so many circumstances had given rise there in his store, for the frequent telling of her history; having incurred, as she had, the hostility of her English speaking black neighbors, at whom she rarely ever glanced. By some strange trick of fortune, these black neighbors were much better off than she, and loved to put their little ones up to poking fun at her whenever she came to the store for the small purchases that she made—beans and rice, almost invariably, with a whispered request for meat-scrapings, thrown in by way of courtesy. Poking their heads in roguishly, thru the half-opened door, these taunting, little urchins were wont to scream at her, "Dere she goes, fellahs, look at 'er. A picayune o' red beans, a picayune o' rice, lagri-cappe salt meat to make it taste nice." Then Mlle. 'Tasie would laugh loudly to hide her embarrassment. Pityingly she would say with up-lifted shoulders and outwardly turned palms, "Ow you ken h-expec' any bettah fum dem? My own fadda h-own plenty lak dat.—But h-I know, me. H-eet ees dey madda, yes, teach 'em lak dat. She ees mad 'cause h-I doan associate wid 'er. But 'er mahster wheep 'er back plenty, yes.

Me—h-I nevva know a mahster, me. H-ask h-any one eef h-eet ees de trufe and dey will tell you."

None knew better of Mlle. 'Tasie's family than Paul Donseigneur, the clothier of Orleans Street. Paul had been owned by Mlle. 'Tasie's father, Jose Gomez, who belonged to that class of mulattoes known before the Civil War as free men of color. Escaping from the island of Guadaloupe, during a West Indian insurrection, Gomez had settled in New Orleans, purchased a number of slaves and a goodly portion of land, ultimately becoming a "rentier" of some importance. Paul, a tailor by trade, had been assigned to the making of his master's clothes. Because of his efficiency and estimable character, he had rapidly risen in favor. But Paul was aspiring also. He longed for his freedom and begged permission of Gomez to purchase it from him. After much deliberation, the latter surprised him one day with a gift of himself,—that is, with free papers showing a complete bestowal of Paul and all that he possessed upon himself.

Paul was deeply grateful. It was not in his nature, as it was with so many of his race, to hate the hand that lifted him, when that hand was black. He never forgot the generosity of his master, nor his subsequent assistance in the way of influence, immediately after the Civil War, toward the foundation of the very business in which he was still engaged.

But times had been precarious in New Orleans for any business venture during the early years of reconstruction. Especially so for Paul, efficient and alert though he was, yet an ex-slave, with no capital and no business experience. During the general upheaval, he saw nothing of his master who, like many men of his class, had kept well out of the way of all danger. When the smoke and powder of wrought-up feelings had at last cleared away, Paul again looked about for his old master, with the hope that things had not gone so badly with him. But alas! There was not the slightest trace of him to be found. Had he left the city, or had he only gone uptown? Either step would have been fatal for Paul's finding him. For people in the Faubourg Ste. Marie—the American quarter—were as completely lost at any time, to the people of the French quarter, as if they had gone to New York.

Paul knew that out of that great family of many sons and daughters, only two remained. At least there had been two when last he saw them—his master and Mlle. 'Tasie, the youngest daughter. How had they fared during all those troublous times? Wherever they were, he knew that they were poorer; for the Civil War had stripped them of most of their possessions, and unprepared as they were for service, they would never be able to retrieve them, he was certain. It was all very sad. But there was nothing to be done, since he knew not where to find them.

Chance, however, some ten years later, just before the opening of our story, discovered to him one member of that family at least, Mlle. 'Tasie. He was crossing over to the French Market, one morning, from the old Place D'Armes, en route to his clothing store, when he heard the guttural tones of a Gascon restaurateur raised in heated discussion. Hastening to the spot he saw seated upon one of the high stools, before the oil cloth-covered counter of the "coffee stand," a shabby, little colored woman in a black calico dress, much-worn but speckless gaiters, and a long, cotton crepe veil thrown back from a faded straw hat—a perfect picture of bitter poverty trying to be genteel.

Thru the cracked and much be-scratched mirror that ran around the wall of the "coffee stand" in front of her, he saw reflected her small pinched face, courageously rouged and powdered, and recognized Mlle. 'Tasie.

Wonderingly, Paul took in the situation. The merchant's prices, it seems, were higher than some of the others in the market, or more, anyhow, than Mlle. 'Tasie had been aware of. When the time came to pay for what she had eaten, small tho' it was, she was unprepared to do so completely. Hence the Gasconian war of words.

Mlle. 'Tasie's embarrassment at the turn of affairs was beyond description. With trembling fingers peeping out from cotton lace mittens that time had worn from black to green, she hurriedly lowered her veil, then fumbled about in her lace-covered reticule as if seeking the desired change with absolute fright. Going forward, Paul touched the enraged Gascon on the elbow. The sight of his proffered coin was like oil poured upon troubled waters. Mlle. 'Tasie was saved.

When she lifted her tearful eyes to Paul's pitying face, he saw even through the faded veil what privation had done for her. Gently he took her by the arm and led her to the Place D'Armes thru which he had but just passed. And there upon one of the benches, he coaxed out of her, her whole tragic story. She told him how their poverty becoming greater and greater, she and her father had hidden themselves as he had feared, in the American quarter across Canal Street, away from the people who had known them in brighter days; of her father's subsequent death, and her struggles to support herself with her needle; of her many failures at doing so, because of her complete unpreparedness. To his reproachful query as to why she had not appealed to him, she had answered, shoulders up-lifted and mitten-covered palms turned outward, "Ow h-I could do dat, my deah? Come wid my 'and h-open to you? Me? H-eet was h-impossible."

But he assured her that the success of his tailoring business, slow, to be sure, but very promising always, was such that he might have aided them at the time and was in a still better position of doing so now. She shook her head sadly at the suggestion, and her tears began to flow anew. "Me, h-I would die first!" she exclaimed passionately, "befo' h-I would come to dat."

When she grew calmer, he told her of an innovation that he was planning to bring into his business—the making of blue jeans into trousers for the roustabouts on the Levee, and for other workmen. She mopped her eyes and looked at him with interest. It was jean trousers, she had told him, that she had been attempting to make ever since she had been a breadwinner. But the factories from which she had taken work to be done at home had been so exacting, "docking" her for every mis-stitch, and every mistake in hemming so that there was always very little money coming to her when she finally brought her work back.

Paul surmised as much but had already thought out a plan to meet the situation. He would put her directly under the seamstress in charge, for supervision and instruction. And so, at length, Mlle. 'Tasie was installed into the business of her former slave. Her backwardness in learning to do the work set before her was, at first, disheartening. But for the sake of "Auld Lang Syne," Paul nerved himself into forbearance. When, at last, she gave evidence of beginning to "get the hang" of it, so to speak, she caught a dreadful cold at that Creole Mardi Gras ball.

For Mlle. 'Tasie was still young enough to long for

pleasure with something of the ardor of her happier days. She was no "spring chicken" she confessed to herself sadly; she was thirty-seven "come nex 'h-All Saints Day," but that did not prevent her from wanting to "h-enjoy herse'f, yes, once een a w'ile h-any 'ow." Since Mardi Gras comes but once a year, she decided to forget everything and go to the ball. Closing her eyes at the horror of the thing—the laying aside of the mourning which she had worn for the past year for an aunt whom she had never seen—she went down into her trunk and pulled out an ancient blue organdy and a thin, white scarf. It had been years since she had seen these things, for some distant relative of Mlle. 'Tasie was always passing away, and custom compelled her to remember them during a long period of mourning.

Perhaps it was her act of rebellion against this custom, she kept telling herself, that had brought such disaster to her health. Oh, if she only had to do it again, how differently would she act. It had meant the almost giving up of her work at Paul Donseigneur's store, for most of her time was now spent at home trying to get well.

Calling one day to ascertain for himself the cause of these frequent absences, Paul became much disturbed at her appearance. She looked more frail than he had ever seen her. Certainly work, he decided, was not what she wanted now, but care and attention. She had already refused from him, in her foolish pride, everything but what she strictly earned by the sweat of her brow. How to help her now in this new extremity was indeed a problem. He must think it out. And Paul left her more perplexed than he had been before.

As he was about to enter his clothing store, he was stopped by a traveling salesman, Titus Johnson, from

166

whom he bought most of the cottonade that he used. Titus was large and black, well-fed and prosperous-looking, with a fat cigar forever in his mouth and a shiny watch-chain forever dangling from his vest. Titus was the idol of his associates, likewise the idol of the "cook-shop" where he ate, for besides ordering the largest and most expensive steaks they carried, together with hot biscuits, rice, French fried potatoes, buckwheat cakes and coffee, he tipped the waiter lavishly and treated him to a cigar besides. Not only generous, but full of good cheer was Titus, his hearty laugh resounding from one end of the street to the other. Especially so after he had told one of his characteristic jokes, which invariably brought as great a laugh from himself as from his listeners. Simple, whole-hearted and kindly, Titus Johnson met the world with a beaming face and received much of its goodwill in return.

"Hey dere, boss," he shouted to Paul from across the narrow street, as the latter stood upon the sill of his odd-looking suit-store. "I ben waitin' for you. W'at kep' you?" In a stride or two he was at Paul's side. "I hope you ain't gotten so prosperous," he continued, "dat you dodgin' us black folks and fixin' ter pass for white. Hya! Hya! Hya! Hya!" His great voice sounded to the end of the block.

"No danger," smiled back Paul, whose physiognomy forbade any such intention. "I been visitin' de sick. An'—"

"De sick? Who's sick?" Titus' face bespoke concern.

"Mlle. 'Tasie," replied Paul, "De lil' lady who use to sit at dat machine dere by de winda."

"Sho' nuff?" Titus knitted his brow. "I knows her. Leastwise, I mean, I seen her time and time again.— An' you say she's sick?—Very sick? You know, I uster lak

167

ter look at dat lil' body. 'Pere lak dere wuz somepun' so pitiful lak, about her."

"Pitiful," reiterated Paul, his face wearing its troubled look. "Mais, it is worse yet. It is trageec."

"You doan say!—She ain' goin' die, is she?"

"Ah, I hope not dat, me.—All de same, she need right now plenty of care, yes. An'—you know, some one to see after her—right." He led the way thru a disordered room where women of various shades of color were bending over their work, some at machines, others at long cutting tables. When at length he reached his crowded little office in another wing of the building, he sank heavily into a chair, and motioned Titus to be seated also.

Why talk of business now, he mused, when his mind was so full of Mlle. 'Tasie, and her problems? She was downright troublesome, to say the least, he decided. Why had she let herself get into that weakened condition, just when she was beginning to earn enough to support herself decently? And she was so foolishly proud! It was absurd, it was ridiculous.

Before he knew it, Paul found himself telling the whole story to Titus Johnson—the history of Mlle. 'Tasie and of her remarkable family. Titus was astounded. He had heard that before the Civil War, New Orleans had held a number of men of his race who had not only been free themselves, but had owned a large number of slaves, but he had thought it only a myth. But here, according to Paul, was a representative of that class. He longed to meet her; to really be able, as he expressed it to Paul, to give her "his compliments." Never had he felt so much interest in any one before. When she got better, if Paul would arrange a meeting between them he would be glad to take her

168

some evening to the Spanish Fort—the great, white way of New Orleans—or to see the Minstrel—some place where she could laugh and forget her troubles.

Titus, like most English-speaking Negroes, felt no inferiority to the better-born of his race, like Mlle. 'Tasie. Had anyone suggested it, he would have scoffed at the possibility of her looking down upon him. For was she not also a Negro? However low his origin, she could never get any higher than he. Her status had been fixed with his by the highest authority.

Paul pondered Titus' proposition. He knew Mlle. 'Tasie's prejudice to color, but he refrained from mentioning it. She was in great extremity and Titus was both prosperous and big-hearted. Suppose a match could be arranged between them in spite of her prejudices. Stranger things than that had happened. Paul was an old man, and had seen women, bigger than Mlle. 'Tasie let go their prejudices under economic stress. When insistently the stomach growls, he mused, and the shoe pinches, women cease to discriminate and take the relief at hand. The thing was worth trying.

Looking up into the eager face of Titus Johnson, Paul promised to arrange a meeting between him and Mlle. 'Tasie at the first possible opportunity. Titus went away highly pleased. Altho he would not have named it so the thing promised an adventure; and, approaching forty tho he was, it was nevertheless very pleasing to contemplate. As for Paul, that man realized with misgiving that there was much preparatory work to be done on Mlle. 'Tasie before the meeting could even be mentioned to her. He, therefore, planned to set about doing so without delay.

But strange to say, when he approached her on the subject, Mlle. 'Tasie was more tractable than he dared hope for. Undoubtedly she had been doing some serious thinking for herself. Here she was, she told herself, rapidly approaching forty, her health broken down, and no help in the way of a husband anywhere in sight. How different it was from what she had dreamed. Long before this, she had thought the "right one" would have turned up—and she would have been settled down for life. But alas! the men she had wanted, had all gone to handsomer and younger women. She had been too discriminating, too exacting. That was her trouble. But all that must stop now. She must feel herself blessed if some well-to-do man, even tho he met but half her requirements, should come along and propose to her.

And so when Paul, after dilating upon the prosperity and bigheartedness of the black "Americain," advised in the most persuasive of language that she permit him to call, instead of flaring up, as he had been sure she would do, she heard him out quietly and consented after a moment or two of sad reflection. Surprised beyond measure at the ready acquiescence, he sat looking at her for a full second in open-mouthed wonderment. Then he congratulated her on her good, common sense; shook hands with her heartily and left, promising to bring Titus as soon as he returned to New Orleans.

But Mlle. 'Tasie's cheerfulness after that seemed to have deserted her. Her health, tho far from being completely restored, enabled her, before long, to resume her duties at the store. And there she sat at her machine, perplexed and miserable, a dumb spectacle of defeat. Since necessity compelled an abandonment of her prejudices, she reflected, if only she could leave the neighborhood before this black man called, so that those who knew her sentiments might not have the pleasure of laughing in her face. But to be compelled to remain right there and receive with a pretense of welcome before a group of peeping, grinning back-biters, the very kind of "Negre aux grosses oreilles" whom she had been known to look down upon—Mon Dieu!—how could one be cheerful after that?

Yet in spite of this dread, the time came at last, when Titus, traveling agent that he was, again arrived in New Orleans. To say that he was eager to meet Mlle. 'Tasie, is far, very far, from the mark, for he fairly lived in the expectation. But Titus was a natural psychologist. On the day of his arrival, contrary to his usual custom, he remained away from Paul's store during the hours that he knew Mlle. 'Tasie was in it, altho he saw to it that Paul got a message that he had not only arrived in town, but would call on Mlle. 'Tasie that evening. For an adventure such as this must not be spoiled thru haste or lack of preparation.

"Ef you wants a lady to 'preciate you," Titus mused, "you must fust have de proper settin'; 'cause settin's everything. You mustn't on'y fix yo'self up for her, but you must git her all worked up fixin' up for you. Den w'en you comes in swaggerin' on yo' cane, a half hour or an hour after she expected you to come, you got her jes' as anxious to meet you, as you is her. All de rest den is clare sailin'."

Arriving in the morning, Titus spent the day shop-ping. Nothing but the newest apparel must meet her eye when first she beheld him. When Paul, therefore, rather falteringly presented him in the evening after having apprised Mlle. 'Tasie much earlier of his expected visit, Titus was resplendent in brand new "malakoff"-bottom trousers, well creased in the middle, a "coffin-back" shaped coat to match, creaking red brogues, lemon colored tie, and a deep red Camellia in the buttonhole of his coat.

To a man less self-conscious than Titus was at the moment, the meeting would have been a dismal failure. For there was nothing of cordiality in Mlle. 'Tasie's subdued and rather mournful greeting. Paul was so impressed by the chilliness of it, that he beat a hasty retreat, leaving Romeo to the winning of his Juliet unaided. And Titus proved that he was not unequal to the task, for he soon had Mlle. 'Tasie interested in spite of herself. He told her of his travels up and down the state, described the dreary islands of Barataria with their secret passages, where smugglers and robbers nearly a hundred years before had hidden their ill-gotten gains. And had a world of news about the folks of Opoulousas and Point Coupee, places she had not visited since she was a girl. When at length he rose to go, she felt something very much like regret, and before she knew it, entirely forgetful of his color, she had invited him to call again.

Not only was Titus' "gift of gab" an asset to his courting but his frequent absences from town as well. For Mlle. 'Tasie could not help but feel the contrast between the quiet, uneventful evenings without him, and the cheer, the jokes, the kindly gossip that filled the hours when he was there. If only she had not to face the "pryers" with explanations as to why she had become suddenly so "cosmopel" as to bring into her home an American of his complexion. Relatives whom she hadn't seen for months hearing of the strangeness of her conduct, came way from Bayou Rouge and Elysian Fields Street to beg her with tears in their eyes not to disgrace them by allying herself with an American "Negre aux grosses oreilles."

172

Mlle. 'Tasie became distracted. The opinion of these people meant much to her; but after long thinking she realized that the protection and assistance of a husband would mean vastly more. So she nerved herself to defiance. When at length, Titus proposed marriage to her, she accepted him, not with any feeling stronger than liking, it is true, but with a sense of great satisfaction that now she was for a truth, to have a protector at last.

But now that the marriage day had arrived she felt all the old hesitancy, the repugnance, the sensitiveness because of what the others had been saying, come back upon her, with painful intensity. Yet, nevertheless, she bravely prepared for the event. When, at length, evening came and her shabby, little parlor where the ceremony took place became enlivened by the cheery presence of Titus and the only two invited guests—Paul and the owner of the "cook-shop" where Titus ate—Mlle. 'Tasie felt herself grow calmer.

After partaking lavishly of her "wine sangeree" and her carefully-prepared tea-cakes, the guests finally took their departure. Titus went up to her and putting both his fat hands upon her shoulders, smiled reassuringly into her eyes. "Well ole 'oman," he said, "you an' me goin' ter make it fine! It's me an' you' gainst de whole worl', you heah me? You po' lil' critter! You needs somebody ter take care o' you, an' Titus Johnson is de one ter take de job." Then Mlle. 'Tasie felt a sort of peace steal over her, the harbinger, she hoped of happier days.

First published in the journal
Opportunity (September 1925)

ALICE DUNBAR-NELSON

Sonnet

I had not thought of violets late,
The wild, shy kind that spring beneath your feet
In wistful April days, when lovers mate
And wander through the fields in raptures sweet.
The thought of violets meant florists' shops,
And bows and pins, and perfumed papers fine;
And garish lights, and mincing little fops
And cabarets and soaps, and deadening wines.
So far from sweet real things my thoughts had
     strayed,
I had forgot wide fields; and clear brown streams;
The perfect loveliness that God has made,—
Wild violets shy and Heaven-mounting dreams.
And now—unwittingly, you've made me dream
Of violets, and my soul's forgotten gleam.

Published in *The Book of American Negro Poetry,* an anthology edited by James Weldon Johnson (1922)

CARRIE WILLIAMS CLIFFORD

Tomorrow

(*"Ethiopia shall stretch forth her hand"*)

Tomorrow! magic word of promise rare,
What witchery inheres in thy sweet name,
Inspiring wild ambition, naught can tame,
To conquer failure—here or otherwhere;
The rosy rapture thou dost ever bear
Upon thy brow, is but the beacon-flame—
The luminous lodestone, luring on to fame
And high endeavor! Simple friend, beware
The fool who says, "Tomorrow—never comes";
For opportunities like bursting bombs
Shall blast the walls that limit us Today.
And *all*, who wish within *its* scope to stay.
Time has no end save in eternity
Of which *Tomorrow* is the prophecy.

First published in Carrie Williams Clifford's
collection *The Widening Light* (1922)

175

M'sieu Fortier's Violin

Slowly, one by one, the lights in the French Opera go out, until there is but a single glimmer of pale yellow flickering in the great dark space, a few moments ago all a-glitter with jewels and the radiance of womanhood and a-clash with music. Darkness now, and silence, and a great haunted hush over all, save for the distant cheery voice of a stage hand humming a bar of the opera.

The glimmer of gas makes a halo about the bowed white head of a little old man putting his violin carefully away in its case with aged, trembling, nervous fingers. Old M'sieu Fortier was the last one out every night.

Outside the air was murky, foggy. Gas and electricity were but faint splotches of light on the thick curtain of fog and mist. Around the opera was a mighty bustle of carriages and drivers and footmen, with a car gaining headway in the street now and then, a howling of names and numbers, the laughter and small talk of cloaked society stepping slowly to its carriages, and the more bourgeoisie vocalisation of the foot passengers who streamed along and hummed little bits of music. The fog's denseness was confusing, too, and at one moment it seemed that the little narrow street would become inextricably choked and remain so until some mighty engine would blow the crowd into atoms. It had been a crowded night. From around Toulouse Street, where led the entrance to the troisièmes, from the grand stairway, from the entrance to the quatrièmes, the human stream poured into the street, nearly all with a song on their lips.

M'sieu Fortier stood at the corner, blinking at the beautiful ladies in their carriages. He exchanged a hearty salutation with the saloon-keeper at the corner, then, tenderly carrying his violin case, he trudged down Bourbon Street, a little old, bent, withered figure, with shoulders shrugged up to keep warm, as though the faded brown overcoat were not thick enough.

Down on Bayou Road, not so far from Claiborne Street, was a house, little and old and queer, but quite large enough to hold M'sieu Fortier, a wrinkled dame, and a white cat. He was home but little, for on nearly every day there were rehearsals; then on Tuesday, Thursday, and Saturday nights, and twice Sundays there were performances, so Ma'am Jeanne and the white cat kept house almost always alone. Then, when M'sieu Fortier was at home, why, it was practice, practice all the day, and smoke, snore, sleep at night. Altogether it was not very exhilarating.

M'sieu Fortier had played first violin in the orchestra ever since—well, no one remembered his not playing there. Sometimes there would come breaks in the seasons, and for a year the great building would be dark and silent. Then M'sieu Fortier would do jobs of playing here and there, one night for this ball, another night for that soirée dansante, and in the day, work at his trade,—that of a cigar-maker. But now for seven years there had been no break in the season, and the little old violinist was happy. There is nothing sweeter than a regular job and good music to play, music into which one can put some soul, some expression, and which one must study to understand. Dance music, of the frivolous, frothy kind deemed essential to soirées, is trivial easy, uninteresting.

So M'sieu Fortier, Ma'am Jeanne, and the white cat lived a peaceful, uneventful existence out on Bayou Road. When the opera season was over in February, M'sieu went back to cigar-making, and the white cat purred none the less contentedly.

It had been a benefit to-night for the leading tenor, and he had chosen "Roland à Ronceveaux," a favourite this season, for his farewell. And, mon Dieu, mused the little M'sieu, but how his voice had rung out bell-like, piercing above the chorus of the first act! Encore after encore was given, and the bravos of the troisièmes were enough to stir the most sluggish of pulses.

> "Superbes Pyrenées
> Qui dressez dans le ciel,
> Vos cimes couronnées
> D'un hiver éternelle,
> Pour nous livrer passage
> Ouvrez vos larges flancs,
> Faîtes taire l' orage,
> Voici, venir les Francs!"

M'sieu quickened his pace down Bourbon Street as he sang the chorus to himself in a thin old voice, and then, before he could see in the thick fog, he had run into two young men.

"I—I—beg your pardon,—messieurs," he stammered.

"Most certainly," was the careless response; then the speaker, taking a second glance at the object of the rencontre, cried joyfully:

"Oh, M'sieu Fortier, is it you? Why, you are so happy, singing your love sonnet to your lady's eyebrow, that you didn't see a thing but the moon, did you? And who is the fair one who should clog your senses so?"

There was a deprecating shrug from the little man.

"Ma foi, but monsieur must know fo' sho', dat I am too old for love songs!"

"I know nothing save that I want that violin of yours. When is it to be mine, M'sieu Fortier?"

"Nevare, nevare!" exclaimed M'sieu, gripping on as tightly to the case as if he feared it might be wrenched from him. "Me a lovere, and to sell mon violon! Ah, so ver' foolish!"

"Martel," said the first speaker to his companion as they moved on up town, "I wish you knew that little Frenchman. He's a unique specimen. He has the most exquisite violin I've seen in years; beautiful and mellow as a genuine Cremona, and he can make the music leap, sing, laugh, sob, skip, wail, anything you like from under his bow when he wishes. It's something wonderful. We are good friends. Picked him up in my French-town rambles. I've been trying to buy that instrument since—"

"To throw it aside a week later?" lazily inquired Martel. "You are like the rest of these nineteenth-century vandals, you can see nothing picturesque that you do not wish to deface for a souvenir; you cannot even let simple happiness alone, but must needs destroy it in a vain attempt to make it your own or parade it as an advertisement."

As for M'sieu Fortier, he went right on with his song and turned into Bayou Road, his shoulders still shrugged high as though he were cold, and into the quaint little house, where Ma'am Jeanne and the white cat, who always waited up for him at nights, were both nodding over the fire.

It was not long after this that the opera closed, and M'sieu went back to his old out-of-season job. But somehow he did not do as well this spring and summer

179

as always. There is a certain amount of cunning and finesse required to roll a cigar just so, that M'sieu seemed to be losing, whether from age or deterioration it was hard to tell. Nevertheless, there was just about half as much money coming in as formerly, and the quaint little pucker between M'sieu's eyebrows which served for a frown came oftener and stayed longer than ever before.

"Minesse," he said one day to the white cat,—he told all his troubles to her; it was of no use to talk to Ma'am Jeanne, she was too deaf to understand,—"Minesse, we are gettin' po'. You' père git h'old, an' hees han's dey go no mo' rapidement, an' dere be no mo' soirées dese day. Minesse, eef la saison don' hurry up, we shall eat ver' lil' meat."

And Minesse curled her tail and purred.

Before the summer had fairly begun, strange rumours began to float about in musical circles. M. Maugé would no longer manage the opera, but it would be turned into the hands of Americans, a syndicate. Bah! These English-speaking people could do nothing unless there was a trust, a syndicate, a company immense and dishonest. It was going to be a guarantee business, with a strictly financial basis. But worse than all this, the new manager, who was now in France, would not only procure the artists, but a new orchestra, a new leader. M'sieu Fortier grew apprehensive at this, for he knew what the loss of his place would mean to him.

September and October came, and the papers were filled with accounts of the new artists from France and of the new orchestra leader too. He was described as a most talented, progressive, energetic young man. M'sieu Fortier's heart sank at the word "progressive."

He was anything but that. The New Orleans Creole blood flowed too sluggishly in his old veins.

November came; the opera reopened. M'sieu Fortier was not re-engaged.

"Minesse," he said with a catch in his voice that strongly resembled a sob, "Minesse, we mus' go hongry sometime. Ah, mon pauvre violon! Ah, mon Dieu, dey put us h'out, an' dey will not have us. Nev' min', we will sing anyhow." And drawing his bow across the strings, he sang in his thin, quavering voice, "Salut demeure, chaste et pure."

It is strange what a peculiar power of fascination former haunts have for the human mind. The criminal, after he has fled from justice, steals back and skulks about the scene of his crime; the employee thrown from work hangs about the place of his former industry; the schoolboy, truant or expelled, peeps in at the school-gate and taunts the good boys within. M'sieu Fortier was no exception. Night after night of the performances he climbed the stairs of the opera and sat, an attentive listener to the orchestra, with one ear inclined to the stage, and a quizzical expression on his wrinkled face. Then he would go home, and pat Minesse, and fondle the violin.

"Ah, Minesse, dose new player! Not one bit can dey play. Such tones, Minesse, such tones! All the time portemento, oh, so ver' bad! Ah, mon chere violon, we can play." And he would play and sing a romance, and smile tenderly to himself.

At first it used to be into the deuxièmes that M'sieu Fortier went, into the front seats. But soon they were too expensive, and after all, one could hear just as well in the fourth row as in the first. After a while even the rear row of the deuxièmes was too costly, and the little

181

musician wended his way with the plebeians around on Toulouse Street, and climbed the long, tedious flight of stairs into the troisièmes. It makes no difference to be one row higher. It was more to the liking, after all. One felt more at home up here among the people. If one was thirsty, one could drink a glass of wine or beer being passed about by the libretto boys, and the music sounded just as well.

But it happened one night that M'sieu could not even afford to climb the Toulouse Street stairs. To be sure, there was yet another gallery, the quatrièmes, where the peanut boys went for a dime, but M'sieu could not get down to that yet. So he stayed outside until all the beautiful women in their warm wraps, a bright-hued chattering throng, came down the grand staircase to their carriages.

It was on one of these nights that Courcey and Martel found him shivering at the corner.

"Hello, M'sieu Fortier," cried Courcey, "are you ready to let me have that violin yet?"

"For shame!" interrupted Martel.

"Fifty dollars, you know," continued Courcey, taking no heed of his friend's interpolation.

M'sieu Fortier made a courtly bow. "Eef Monsieur will call at my 'ouse on de morrow, he may have mon violon," he said huskily; then turned abruptly on his heel, and went down Bourbon Street, his shoulders drawn high as though he were cold.

When Courcey and Martel entered the gate of the little house on Bayou Road the next day, there floated out to their ears a wordless song thrilling from the violin, a song that told more than speech or tears or gestures could have done of the utter sorrow and desolation of the little old man. They walked softly up the short red brick walk and tapped at the door. Within, M'sieu Fortier was caressing the violin, with silent tears streaming down his wrinkled gray face.

There was not much said on either side. Courcey came away with the instrument, leaving the money behind, while Martel grumbled at the essentially sordid, mercenary spirit of the world. M'sieu Fortier turned back into the room, after bowing his visitors out with old-time French courtliness, and turning to the sleepy white cat, said with a dry sob:

"Minesse, dere's only me an' you now."

About six days later, Courcey's morning dreams were disturbed by the announcement of a visitor. Hastily doing a toilet, he descended the stairs to find M'sieu Fortier nervously pacing the hall floor.

"I come fo' bring back you' money, yaas. I cannot sleep, I cannot eat, I only cry, and t'ink, and weesh fo' mon violon; and Minesse, an' de ol' woman too, dey mope an' look bad too, all for mon violon. I try fo' to use dat money, but eet burn an' sting lak blood money. I feel lak' I done sol' my child. I cannot go at l'opera no mo', I t'ink of mon violon. I starve befo' I live widout. My heart, he is broke, I die for mon violon."

Courcey left the room and returned with the instrument.

"M'sieu Fortier," he said, bowing low, as he handed the case to the little man, "take your violin; it was a whim with me, a passion with you. And as for the money, why, keep that too; it was worth a hundred dollars to have possessed such an instrument even for six days."

First published in Alice Dunbar-Nelson's collection, *The Goodness of St Rocque and Other Stories* (1899)

Song

I am weaving a song of waters,
Shaken from firm, brown limbs,
Or heads thrown back in irreverent mirth.
My song has the lush sweetness
Of moist, dark lips
Where hymns keep company
With old forgotten banjo songs.
Abandon tells you
That I sing the heart of a race
While sadness whispers
That I am the cry of a soul . . .

A-shoutin' in de ole camp-meetin-place,
A-strummin' o' de ole banjo.
Singin' in de moonlight,
Sobbin' in de dark.
Singin', sobbin', strummin' slow . . .
Singin' slow, sobbin' low.
Strummin', strummin', strummin' slow . . .
Words are bright bugles
That make the shining for my song,
And mothers hold brown babes
To dark, warm breasts
To make my singing sad.

A dancing girl with swaying hips
Sets mad the queen in a harlot's eye.
      Praying slave
      Jazz-band after

Breaking heart
        To the time of laughter . . .
Clinking chains and minstrelsy
Are welded fast with melody.
        A praying slave
        With a jazz-band after . . .
        Singin' slow, sobbin' low.
Sun-baked lips will kiss the earth.
Throats of bronze will burst with mirth.
        Sing a little faster,
        Sing a little faster,
        Sing!

First published in *The New Negro*,
                an anthology edited by
                Alain Locke (May 1925)

The Wrong Man

The room blazed with color. It seemed that the gorgeous things which the women were wearing had for this once managed to subdue the strident tones of the inevitable black and white of the men's costumes. Tonight they lent just enough of preciseness to add interest to the riotously hued scene. The place was crowded but cool, for a gentle breeze blew from the Sound through the large open windows and doors, now and then stirring some group of flowers.

Julia Romley, in spite of the smoke-colored chiffon gown (ordered specially for the occasion) which she was wearing, seemed even more flamingly clad than the rest. The pale indefinite gray but increased the flaring mop of her hair; scarlet, a poet had called it. The satiny texture of her skin seemed also to reflect in her cheeks a cozy tinge of that red mass.

Julia, however, was not happy tonight. A close observer would have said that she was actively disturbed. Faint abstraction, trite remarks nervously offered, and uncontrolled restlessness marred her customary perfect composure. Her dreamy gray eyes stole frequently in the direction of Myra Redmon's party. Myra always had a lion in tow, but why that particular man? She shook a little as she wondered.

Suddenly, the orchestra blared into something wild and impressionistic, with a primitive staccato understrain of jazz. The buzz of conversation died, strangled by the savage strains of the music. The crowd stirred, broke, coalesced into twos, and became a whirling mass. A partner claimed Julia and they became part of the swaying mob.

"Some show, what?" George Hill's drawling voice was saying, while he secretly wondered what had got into Julia; she was so quiet, not like herself at all.

Julia let her eyes wander over the moving crowd. Young men, old men, young women, older women, slim girls, fat women, thin men, stout men, glided by. The old nursery rhyme came into her mind. She repeated it to George in a singsong tone:

> "Rich man, poor man,
> Beggar man, thief,
> Doctor, lawyer,
> Indian chief."

George nodded. "Yes, that's it. Everybody's here and a few more. And look, look! There's the 'Indian chief.' Wonder who he is? He certainly looks the part."

Julia didn't look; she knew what she would see. A tall, thin man, his lean face yellowed and hardened as if by years in the tropics; a man, perhaps, a bit unused to scenes of this kind, purposely a little aloof and, one suspected, more than a little contemptuous.

She felt a flash of resentful anger against Myra. Why was she always carting about impossible people? It was disgusting. It was worse—it was dangerous. Certainly it was about to become dangerous to her, Julia Romley, erstwhile . . . She let the thought die unfinished, it was too unpleasant.

She had been so happy, so secure, and now this: Ralph Tyler, risen from the past to shatter the happiness which she had grasped for herself. Must she begin all over again? She made a hasty review of her life since San Francisco days: Chicago and the art school where she had studied interior decorating with the money that Ralph Tyler had given her; New York, her studio and success; Boston, and marriage to Jim Romley. And now this envied gay life in one of Long Island's most exclusive sets. Yes, life had been good to her at last, better than she had ever dreamed. Was she about to lose everything—love, wealth, and position? She shivered.

"Cold?" Again George's drawling voice dragging her back to the uncertain present.

"No, not cold. Just someone walking over my grave," she answered laughingly. "I'm rotten company tonight, George. I'm sorry; I'll do better. It's the crowd, I guess."

Her husband claimed her for the next dance. A happy married pair, their obvious joy in each other after five wedded years was the subject of amused comment and mild jokes among their friends. "The everlasting lovers," they were dubbed, and the name suited them as perfectly as they suited each other.

"What's wrong, Julie, old girl?" asked Jim after a few minutes' baffled scrutiny. "Tired?"

"Nothing, nothing. I just feel small, so futile in this crush; sort of trapped, you know. Why *do* the Arnolds have so many people to their things?" Quickly regretting her display of irritation, she added: "It's wonderful, though—the people, the music, the color, and these lovely rooms, like a princess's ball in a fairy tale."

"Yes, great," he agreed. "Lots of strangers here, too; most of them distinguished people from town."

"Who's the tall browned man with Myra, who looks like—well, like an Indian chief?" She laughed a little at her own pleasantry, just to show Jim that there was nothing troubling her.

"Doesn't he, though? Sort of self-sufficient and superior and a bit indifferent, as if he owned us all and despised the whole tribe of us. I guess you can't blame him much. He probably thinks we're a soft, lazy, self-pampering lot. He's Ralph Tyler, an explorer, just back from some godforsaken place on the edge of nowhere. Been head of some expedition lost somewhere in Asia for years, given up for dead. Discovered a buried city or something; great contribution to civilization and all that, you know. They say he brought back some emeralds worth a king's ransom."

"Do you know him, Jim?"

"Yes; knew him years ago in college. Didn't think he'd remember me after such a long time and all those thrilling adventures, but he did. Honestly, you could have knocked me over with a feather when he came over to me and put out his hand and said, 'Hello there, Jim Romley.' Nice, wasn't it?" Jim's handsome face glowed. He was undoubtedly flattered by the great man's remembrance. He went on enthusiastically: "I'm going to have him out to the house, Julie; that is, if I can get him. Small, handpicked dinner party. What say?"

She shivered again.

"Cold?"

"No, not cold. Just someone walking over my grave." She laughed, amused at the double duty of the superstition in one evening, and glad too that Jim had not noticed that his question had passed unanswered.

Dance followed dance. She wasn't being a success tonight. She knew it, but somehow she couldn't make small talk. Her thoughts kept wandering to that tall browned man who had just come back from the world's end. One or two of her partners, after trying in vain to draw her out, looked at her quizzically, wondering if the impossible had happened. Had Julia and old Jim quarreled?

At last she escaped to a small deserted room on an upper floor, where she could be alone to think. She groped about in her mind for some way to avoid that dinner party. It spelled disaster. She must find some way to keep Ralph Tyler from finding out that she was the wife of his old schoolmate. But if he were going to be here for any length of time, and Jim seemed to think that he would, she would have to meet him. Perhaps she could go away? . . . No, she dared not; anything might happen. Better to be on hand to ward off the blow when it fell. She sighed, suddenly weary and beaten. It was hopeless. And she had been so happy! Just a faint shadow of uneasiness, at first, which had gradually faded as the years slipped away.

She sat for a long time in deep thought. Her face settled into determined lines; she made up her mind. She would ask, plead if necessary, for his silence. It was the only way. It would be hard, humiliating even, but it must be done if she were to continue to be happy in Jim's love. She couldn't bear to look ahead to years without him.

She crossed the room and wrote a note to Ralph Tyler, asking him to meet her in the summerhouse in one of the gardens. She hesitated a moment over the signature, finally writing *Julia Hammond*, in order to prepare him a little for the meeting.

After she had given the note into the hand of a servant for delivery "to Mr. Tyler, the man with Mrs. Redmon," she experienced a slight feeling of relief. "At least I can try," she thought as she made her way to the summerhouse to wait. "Surely, if I tell him about myself and Jim, he'll be merciful."

★

The man looked curiously at the woman sitting so motionless in the summerhouse in the rock garden. Even in the darkness she felt his gaze upon her, though she lacked the courage to raise her eyes to look at him. She waited expectantly for him to speak.

After what seemed hours but was, she knew, only seconds, she understood that he was waiting for her to break the silence. So she began to speak in a low hesitating voice:

"I suppose you think it strange, this request of mine to meet me here alone; but I had to see you, to talk to you. I wanted to tell you about my marriage to Jim Romley. You know him?"

"Yes, I know him."

"Well," she went on, eagerly now, "you see, we're so happy! Jim's so splendid, and I've tried to be such a good wife. And I thought—I thought—you see, I thought—" The eager voice trailed off on a note of entreaty.

"Yes, you thought?" prompted the man in a noncommittal tone.

"Well, you see, I thought that if you knew how happy we were, and how much I love him, and that since you know Jim, that you—you—"

She stopped. She couldn't go on, she simply couldn't. But she must. There he stood like a long, menacing shadow between her and the future. She began again, this time with insinuating flattery:

"You have so much yourself now—honor, fame, and money—and you've done such splendid things! You've suffered too. How you must have suffered! Oh, I'm glad of your success; you deserve it. You're a hero, a great man. A little thing like that can't matter to you now and it means everything to me, everything. Please spare me my little happiness. Please be kind!"

"But I don't understand." The man's voice was puzzled. "How 'kind'? What is it you're asking?"

Reading masked denial in the question, Julia began to sob softly.

"Don't tell Jim! Please, don't tell Jim! I'll do anything to keep him from knowing, anything."

"But aren't you making a mistake? I—"

"Mistake?" She laughed bitterly. "I see; you think I should have told him. You think that even now I should tell him that I was your mistress once. You don't know Jim. He'd never forgive that. He wouldn't understand that, when a girl has been sick and starving on the streets, anything can happen to her; that she's greateful for food and shelter at any price. You won't tell him, will you?"

"But I'm sure," stammered the tall figure, fumbling for cigarettes, "I'm sure you've made a mistake. I'm sorry. I've been trying to—"

Julia cut him off. She couldn't bear to hear him speak the refusing words, his voice seemed so grimly final. She knew it was useless, but she made a last desperate effort:

"I was so young, so foolish, and so hungry; but Jim wouldn't understand." She choked over the last words.

He shook his head—impatiently, it seemed to the agonized woman.

"Mrs. Romley, I've been trying to tell you that you've made a mistake. I'm sorry. However, I can assure you that your secret is safe with me. It will never be from my lips that Jim Romley hears you have been—er—what you say you have been."

Only the woman's sharply drawn quivering breath

indicated that she had heard. A match blazed for a moment as he lighted his cigarette with shaking hands. Julia's frightened eyes picked out his face in the flickering light. She uttered a faint dismayed cry.

She had told the wrong man.

First published in *Young's Magazine* (January 1926)

At April

Toss your gay heads,
    Brown girl trees;
Toss your gay lovely heads;
Shake your downy russet curls
All about your brown faces;
Stretch your brown slim bodies;
Stretch your brown slim arms;
Stretch your brown slim toes.
Who knows better than we
With the dark, dark bodies,
What it means
When April comes a-laughing and a-weeping
Once again
At our hearts?

His Great Career

The travel-scarred motorcar came to a pause in the driveway of the great mountain mansion. "The Squire," as he was lovingly called for miles around, greeted the owner of the car as he rather stiffly set foot on the ground.

"It's good of you to come up here to see us in our mountain fastness," he said warmly.

"Didn't know you lived here until we broke down somewhere in your peaks and crags, and Martin inquired of the nearest civilized house."

The Squire talked cheerfully as he carried the bags of the great criminal lawyer up the broad walk.

"We're having a big house party here," he explained the group of guests on the veranda. "My wife's birthday, and when we give a party up here, it means a weekend stay, for we have to go so far for our festivities, it would be a pity to go right home."

The great lawyer was introduced to the fluttering and flattered group of maidens and wives, and to the hearty men who hovered on the edges. He bent his great grizzled fame over small eager hands, while his host stood by, enjoying his embarrassment in the pause before he went to his room.

"And so you're married?" asked the lawyer, as they went up the broad stairs.

"Fifteen years. You remember when my health broke eighteen years ago? I found *her* here in a sanitarium, wrecked too, and 'sick of that disease called life.' Between us, we mended our lives, and then she didn't care for the east and all that it means any more than I did—so we stayed, and here we are."

The great lawyer revelled in the scene, a marvelous panorama spreading out from the window.

"Prominent citizen, leader of the community, and the rest?" he asked smilingly.

The Squire was modest. "Well, we've helped build the community, and all that sort of thing. You can't live in a place without being part of it. And you, old Hardhead, you've become one of the most famous lawyers in the country!"

The lawyer waved a deprecating hand. "I'm motoring in out of the way places now to forget it awhile."

The veranda was not in a mood to allow him to forget. Famous celebrities did not drop into their lives often enough for them to be blasé. The lawyer put down the excellent cocktail that his host brought him in lieu of tea, and inquired for the mistress of the house. She had ridden to town for a last bit of foolery for tonight's costume party, explained the Squire.

The almond-eyed widow was subtly intent on opening up a flood of reminiscences. She fluttered slender hands and widened black eyes suggestively. Even the great lawyer's habitual taciturnity relaxed under the enveloping warmth of remembering the night she had sworn to be avenged on the slim, pale woman, who had taken him, her legitimate prey. A wife and a widow since, but the almond eyes still avid for vengeance.

"You must have had some interesting experiences, have you not? Oh, do tell us about some of your early struggles."

196

The great lawyer expanded under the enveloping perfume of her incense.

"Well," he began, his great voice booming softly in the mountain sunlight, "I shall never forget my first case. I was a briefless barrister, and hungry, or I would not have taken it. Everyone concerned in the affair is dead now, so I can smile at it. My first client was a murderer, a woman. She confessed the truth to me, and expected me to clear her."

"And did you?" chorused an octave of soprano voices.

"Yes. It was the beginning of my career."

A soft intake of breath from the window, and a flattering flutter from the rest of the veranda left the great lawyer to turn to his host.

But the Squire was oblivious, for coming up the walk was the mistress of the mansion. His soul was in his eyes as he watched her. Her eyes glowed, and her face was wind-whipped from riding; she had taken off her hat and her packages dangled from her arm. The lawyer stood in intent stillness. The same lithe form. The same aureole of auburn hair, as yet untinged by gray. The same still, quiet little face with deep pools of eyes. The same questioning droop of head. She came quickly up the walk and onto the veranda with incredible lightness.

"My dear," said the Squire, his voice a protecting caress, "this is—"

But she extended her hand smilingly to the great lawyer, grasping his with welcoming warmth.

"I did not die, you see," she said in her deep, vibrant voice. "The west gave me health and happiness," and still holding his hand with proprietary grasp, she turned to the group on the veranda.

"Mr. Booth is an old friend of mine, too. You see, I was his very first client, and I flatter myself that I started him on his great career."

Unpublished (*c.* 1928–1932)

Further Reading

Marita Bonner, 'On Being Young—a Woman—and Colored', in *Double-Take: A Revisionist Harlem Renaissance Anthology*, Venetria K. Patton and Maureen Honey eds., (New Brunswick, NJ: Rutgers University Press, 2001), p. 112.

Amanda Gorman, *The Hill We Climb: An Inaugural Poem* (New York: Viking, 2021).

Maureen Honey ed., *Shadowed Dreams: Women's Poetry of the Harlem Renaissance* (New Brunswick, New Jersey: Rutgers University Press, 1999).

Maureen Honey, *Aphrodite's Daughters: Three Modernist Poets of the Harlem Renaissance* (New Brunswick, NJ: Rutgers University Press, 2016).

Gloria T. Hull, *Color, Sex, & Poetry: Three Women Writers of the Harlem Renaissance* (Bloomington, IN: Indiana University Press, 1987).

Gloria T. Hull, *Give Us Each Day: The Diary of Alice Dunbar-Nelson* (New York: W. W. Norton, 1984).

June Jordan, 'White English/Black English: The Politics of Translation', *Moving Towards Home: Political Essays* (New York: Virago, 1967).

Marcy Knopf ed., *The Sleeper Wakes: Harlem Renaissance Stories by Women* (New Brunswick, NJ: Rutgers University Press, 1993).

Judith Musser, 'African American Women's Short Stories in the Harlem Renaissance: Bridging a Tradition,' *MELUS*, vol. 23, no. 2 (Summer 1998).

Lorraine Elena Roses and Ruth Elizabeth Randolph eds., *Harlem Renaissance and Beyond: Literary Biographies of 100 Black Women Writers 1900–1945* (Cambridge, MA: Harvard University Press, 1990).

Lorraine Elena Roses and Ruth Elizabeth Roses eds., *Harlem's Glory: Black Women Writing, 1900–1950* (Cambridge, MA: Harvard University Press, 1996).

Cheryl A. Wall, *Women of the Harlem Renaissance* (Bloomington, IN: Indiana University Press, 1995).

Belinda Wheeler and Louis J. Parascandola eds., *Heroine of the Harlem Renaissance and Beyond: Gwendolyn Bennett's Selected Writings* (University Park, PA: Pennsylvania State University Press, 2018).

Permissions Acknowledgements

The lines by Amanda Gorman on p. xix are from *The Hill We Climb*, first published by Chatto & Windus 2021.

'Motherhood', 'Your World' and 'Escape' by Georgia Douglas Johnson; 'Heritage', 'To Usward' and 'Song' by Gwendolyn Bennett; 'At April' by Angelina Weld Grimké from *Shadowed Dreams: Women's Poetry of the Harlem Renaissance* ed. Maureen Honey (2006) published with permission from the Copyright Clearance Centre on behalf of Rutgers University Press.

'The Closing Door' by Angelina Weld Grimké and 'Nothing New' by Marita Bonner from *The Sleeper Wakes* ed. Marcy Knopf Newman (1993) published with permission from the Copyright Clearance Centre on behalf of Rutgers University Press.

MACMILLAN COLLECTOR'S LIBRARY

**Own the world's great works of literature in
one beautiful collectible library**

Designed and curated to appeal to book lovers everywhere,
Macmillan Collector's Library editions are small enough to
travel with you and striking enough to take pride of place
on your bookshelf. These much-loved literary classics
also make the perfect gift.

Beautifully produced with gilt edges, a ribbon marker,
bespoke illustrated cover and real cloth binding, every
Macmillan Collector's Library hardback adheres to the
same high production values.

Discover something new or cherish your favourite
stories with this elegant collection.

**Macmillan Collector's Library:
own, collect, and treasure**

Discover the full range at
macmillancollectorslibrary.com